The Rain Prayer

The Rain Prayer

❖

A Journey Into Becoming A Prayer Warrior

Suzan Michele Powers

iUniverse, Inc.

New York Lincoln Shanghai

The Rain Prayer
A Journey Into Becoming A Prayer Warrior

iUniverse, Inc.

For information address:
iUniverse, Inc.
2021 Pine Lake Road, Suite 100
Lincoln, NE 68512
www.iuniverse.com

ISBN: 0-595-27670-9

Printed in the United States of America

"Everything is possible for him who believes."

—Mark 9:23

This book is dedicated to all people who are on the path of faith or looking for it.

"They will neither harm nor destroy
on all my holy mountain,
for the earth will be full of the
knowledge of the LORD
as waters cover the sea."

—Isaiah 11:9

Contents

Acknowledgments

o o o o o o o o o o o o o o o o o o o o o o o o o o o o o o o o o o
"Blessed are they who hunger
and thirst for righteousness,
for they will be filled."

—Matthew 5:6

I would like to express my gratitude to all the clergy and Christian laity, the law enforcement personnel, medical social service organizations that guided and supported me throughout my ordeal and spiritual enlightenment.

For the Word of knowledge, someone prayed for me because I felt it and it sent me out to a bookstore where I found the brochure that advertised my publisher. Thank you Lord.

This story is based upon true experiences. The names have been changed to protect the innocent.

Preface

"And the Spirit of God was hovering over the waters."

—Genesis 1:1

The names of everyone mentioned in this book have been changed to protect people. The dates and locations are accurate. I believe that events like these can and are happening anywhere and not for any logical reason but to spread terror into our lives. Knowledge and prayer are powerful defenses that we have available to us. Knowledge is a key to dismantling the power of terror over us. When reason fails prayer will sustain and by faith in God we will triumph. The most powerful counter-terrorist activity I found is prayer and the greatest counter-terrorist is Jesus Christ.

I hope this book will help others to understand what I came to understand about God, prayer, and faith. I wrote this book to help people believe that we are not alone and no matter how big or little the terrors are that invade our lives, that we will be reconciled to God and He will bring us closer to His love and peace through prayer in Christ.

I try to make my life a reason to believe in Jesus Christ, our Savior, a witness for the faith. No matter how deep sin cuts into our very soul, the greatest rescue is underway to keep us in the Lord's love and state of grace and through forgiveness and reconciliation we will live forever in His Glory. I thank God for His wisdom and love over us.

I started taping my thoughts for this book in the middle of my turmoil during Desert Storm in 1991. When I began writing in 2000, I wanted to publish my prayer book. I had to stand back when our country was attacked in 2001 and was encouraged by an editor to include 9/11 in my manuscript. It took a year to do that because the trauma was so great I could not assimilate into my writing. I was

xiv   The Rain Prayer

writing a prayer book, a response to the jihad against my country but I was also suffering from ptsd. The courage that I witnessed in the victims, the survivors, families, friends, and the officials helped inspire me. Now we are on the road to freedom in Iraq and hopefully from jihad and this is when *The Rain Prayer* should be published, it is a labor of love.

"I looked, and there before me was a white cloud, and seated on the cloud was one "like a son of man" with a crown of gold on his head and a sharp sickle in his hand. Then another angel came out of the temple and called in a loud voice to him who was sitting on the cloud. "Take your sickle and reap, because the time to reap has come, for the harvest of the earth is ripe. So he who was seated on the cloud swung his sickle over the earth, and the earth was harvested."

Revelation 14:14

1

9/11 Revelation

○ ○
"I am the way, and the truth and the life. No one comes to the Father except through Me."

—John 14:6

"Behold, God's dwelling is with the human race. He will dwell with them and they will be His people and God himself will always be with them.
He will wipe every tear from their eyes, and there shall be no more death or mourning, wailing or pain, the old order has passed away."

—Revelations 21:3-4

September 11, 2001 began like any other Monday in the United States. I was in an unusual place, staying in my ex-in-laws' guest cottage while I was visiting my daughter, son-in-law, and grandchildren. My children didn't have room for me overnight in their farmhouse down the road and felt I would be more comfortable in the roomy guesthouse instead of sleeping on the couch with the dogs and kids waking up in the night because Grandma was there.

My habit of turning on the television as soon as I awake to the "Today" show carried into my vacation. I clicked it on at around 8:50 am to see the most shocking thing I have ever seen on tv. Billowing smoke pouring out of the one of the tallest buildings in the world, one of the Trade Towers, practically knocked my breath out of my body. I was transfixed standing in front of the set, then my mind raced to adjust to what it was. This was an accident I was sure, or was I? In

1

the back of my mind I thought it could be something to do with terrorism. The World Trade Towers had been bombed before. But no, I adjusted my thinking to what my civilized background and education had taught me. This was the United States of America and this was one of the important Trade Towers. I thought in a flash remembering back to a happy vacation my young daughter and my neighbor and her son and I had taken which included New York City. They had never been there. We saw many things there, going to museums, the UN Building, a Broadway play. When I drove past the Trade Towers I asked if anyone wanted to go up to the top. Our mouths dropped open as we crooked our necks up to try to look at the top of the buildings. Everyone responded with a "No!" I felt the same. Now, here in front of me was one of these enormous fortresses on fire and encompassed with huge clouds of thick, black smoke. Then I realized my body was slipping into tremors.

I tried to call my daughter on the cell phone they gave me but it didn't work. The television commentators' voices floated out of the set and all I could hear is that the building had been hit probably by an airplane, they could not confirm. I looked at the picture. It was a crystal clear blue sky day in New York and also clear where I was in Illinois.

I quickly got dressed and went back to the television, standing in front of it monitoring my shallow breathing when out of the beautiful blue sky came a huge jet, flying so big, so close and then smashes into the other Trade Tower. I have to sit down. I know we are under attack. I remember just before I was to fly out of California for my visit, the Presidio in Monterey, California was in a "Charlie" alert. That meant that everyone entering through its gates was security checked. The Presidio is where the Defense Language Institute is located and where CIA and military intelligence training takes place. I had gone out with one of the agents that worked there when I lived in Monterey. I have never been intimidated by it like some people but rather just the opposite; so glad these people were around. However, I had never seen a security alert at the Presidio and it was alarming. Later, I was to find out that the FBI and the CIA were holding a big conference at the Presidio during the very week I was visiting with my daughter's family, the week of 9/11.

Another thought that was taking hold of my mind was how would I get home? Would air traffic stop? Would it be too dangerous? The train popped up or the bus, but the scene on the tv crowded all thoughts of return home out as the two tallest buildings in New York were burning. Tears welled up, tears for the people in the buildings, tears for America, tears for the world, tears for God. I watched the black smoke as little flecks started to drop off the side of the buildings. They were people. People were on fire, holding hands, later to be blocked off the screen because it was too upsetting. The show announcer was anxiously speaking about what was happening. But my mind was tunneling backwards in time, back ten years to when a man spoke to me the most startling words I had ever heard. He said, "We are the call of the jihad, the call of the 20 nations. We will end Israel forever." I watched the burning buildings, the people falling, the screams on the ground, and the nervous commentators with shocked looks on their faces. Everyone in the world would now know "the jihad", I was sure.

My son-in-law arrived to whisk me away to their farm and a fun day with my grandchildren. He had a hot cup of coffee with just the right amount of milk ready for me. God had answered my prayers when my daughter married Michael. I asked him if he had heard the news about the planes crashing in New York. He said that he had and commented quietly about how awful it was to see on tv. They lived a short distance from where I staying so we were there in no time. I walked in with my coffee to the television on with the terrible news. The children were buzzing around as usual, ready to play with Grandma. I was not very good at playing with them that morning; something that I looked forward to because they are so much fun for me to be around. My son-in-law worked nights and Christine had the week off while I was visiting. I was so glad to be with them.

I was glued to the set. We watched until the buildings melted down; the people on the ground running and screaming through the horrible gray smoke and particles of what was once the most vital business center in the world swirling through the air. It was like watching a sci-fi movie. Beyond total comprehension, my mind could not keep taking it all in and my body was growing cold inside from the shocking events I was witnessing. It was near noon when Michael walked into the living room and spoke in his quiet, calming voice that the television would be turned off for the rest of the day because the children were becoming upset by the images and words that were coming from it. I looked up and spoke something in agreement and was relieved when the wave of silence invaded the air followed by the sweet sounds of the children at play.

Later that day we talked about how I would get home. I called the train station and the buses. They were already booked solid for over a week ahead. Then I made the decision to use my plane ticket and fly home as scheduled. We all agreed that would be best.

Michael suddenly wanted to display our country's flag. He had an enormous one that covered the roof when he was finished. We all stood outside to marvel at the house quietly standing in the country air with our beloved red, white and blue flag over most of its roof, bravely proclaiming to all who saw from above as well as from the road that we were Americans.

Nights, when I would return to the cottage, I would switch on the tv to catch the news about what was happening in New York and to learn more about what was the cause of this horrific tragedy. The stories of heroism were unending. The bravery of the people on the hijacked planes that crashed in Pennsylvania, and that crashed into the Pentagon was moving beyond words. Who knows where these planes' targets were. If the Pentagon was the target, they were able to keep it from causing greater damage. Everyone knows now how the bravery of the people on the plane that crashed in Pennsylvania forced it down in the middle of nowhere. The greatness of the New York fire departments and police buoyed me upon the Holy Spirit as I think most of the country was, as we watched the people of this city pull together. The families of the victims in the planes shone with courage to our nation as the stories unfolded of extreme daring on board the doomed planes. The families' strength as the nation watched their grief was inspirational as was the rally of the people of our country to the aid of these families with generous gifts of money.

I was grateful to be with my family as we absorbed the shock waves together. By the end of the week, my daughter wanted to have a candlelight prayer vigil outside with the children. Michael was at work. I filmed it as we prayed for the Lord to watch over our nation as He comforts the families of the victims who are in heaven.

My day of departure arrived and I left in the darkness of pre-dawn for the airport. I arrived three hours early like the newscasts had said to do. There were armed national guards throughout O'Hare, something I had never seen. I was grateful they were there. When I approached the ticket counter, it was as if they almost knew I was coming and booked me on the very next flight. I was boarded and in my seat within an hour of arriving and in the air on my way home two hours ahead of my scheduled departure.

I had asked for an aisle seat because on the flight to visit my daughter, my "gills" were turning green as I looked out the window, something I had never experienced before. I remembered one of my bosses for whom I used to schedule flight reservations almost every week always asked for an aisle seat. The wisdom of the choice was clear to me now. Also I rented a movie. So with my eyes and ears occupied with a cute movie, I barely noticed the two male passengers that could not stay in their seats, pacing the aisles and finally finished the flight standing by their seats with frightened and anxious looks on their faces.

The ground felt so wonderful when we landed. I called everyone when I arrived home safe and sound; telling them how I was whisked through the airport to the plane and in no time was in the air.

I spent the next few weeks watching the news for any information about the terrorists' attacks. As the pieces of the grisly puzzle were put into place by newscasters and government officials, I realized that I was unwillingly tied into the meaning of what had happened. It was the unfolding of an ugly prediction that had been told to me ten years earlier, in a small coastal town in California during the Gulf War. What we can all say now, "The jihad" was in full force. It was a word I had stumbled over and one that our government was not familiar with either in 1991. Now, I was hearing it several times a day. The jihad was a Muslim Holy War.

I am grateful for being able to learn more about what it was that came at me in 1991. Ignorance is not bliss. Religious leaders and scholars, government officials, newscasters began to search through our knowledge about what jihad is, and what terrorism is in general, and why we are targets as citizens of a free country.

The next chapters are dedicated to this story of the announcement of the jihad and what it has meant in my life and how that war cry has led me to a closer relationship with God. Knowledge is the key to strength and prayer the answer to questions that are only now being answered after a decade.

2

The Call

o o o o o o o o o o o o o o o o o o o o o o o o o o o o o o o o o o o o o

"Hear me, O coastlands, listen, O distant peoples."

—*Isaiah 49:1*

Sanctuary: Noun, plural sanctuaries (Middle English sanctuarie, from Middle French sainctuarie, from Late Latin sanctuaruim from Latin sanctus) (14th century) 1. consecrated place 2. a place of refuge and protection

I have tried to understand for many years now why these frightful things I write about happened to me. I have talked it over with friends, with official investigators, with psychologists and doctors, and I still cannot come to a rational conclusion. I thought that maybe one of the reasons was that I am an artist and an American painter on the international level. I paint things that I feel inside and my work was getting international attention, winning awards in juried competitions. I had painted a painting protesting a bombing of a jet that killed many young Americans returning home from Europe. It was a ludicrous attempt to try to understand why it happened. That was the theme of the painting, unjustified revenge that was portrayed as madness with a mystical aspect. I titled it "The Sultaness of the Sea", an impossible title with mystical ties to ancient Arabia. It was my statement about the kind of revenge in women that led to this tragedy. The Sultaness was on a magic carpet ride not a prayer carpet.

Terrorists were blamed for the horrific act, which killed many young American college students. Very briefly, in the newspaper, was an article that made the suggestion that the bombing was an act of revenge. Women in the Middle East were angry because they had lost children in a plane crash that was declared an accident; a plane they believed was brought down my U.S. forces or Western forces. I lived to see the terrorists brought to trial and justice before the world. I knew the grieving families left behind found some closure in their lives. But they probably will always miss their loved ones like I miss my dad, who was killed in a car wreck when I was a baby, every day of my life. I thought of the Muslim women and girls I have met in the United States through my education and later through teaching. They were so beautiful and bright. It was impossible to think of them in the same vein as the women who were being blamed for this vengeful act on innocents. I knew these people were good and honest and would never think of such a horrific act.

The main focus of the body of my work was environmental, an issue that I have been preoccupied with since I was a freshman in high school back in 1962 when the whooping cranes were declared endangered. By 1989 I was specifically celebrating the coming federal recognition of the marine life sanctuaries. My home was on the coast of the sanctuary in California where environmentalists, artists, poets, scientists, politicians, and concerned citizens all were energized by this event. I was busy writing and reciting poetry, and painting and exhibiting, centering on this event of instituting the official protection of wildlife in this sanctuary, of simply recognizing that this was a "sanctuary". It was thrilling and people were being drawn together from counties all around. My social profile was at a higher level than usual because of my environmental and artistic activities. Could this be the reason that targeted me by a network of lurking enemies? This positive energy I was surrounded by was like a shield. I had no negative intuitive feelings and my life was soaring on hope for the future as the country worked on a renewal of our resources.

Perhaps the reason for the events that I am about to explain is because I had been selected as a Professional Artist in the Schools and that created a profile. Maybe it's ironic but the truth was I had left teaching and was working in business back east in Boston when I was inspired to return to education. Teaching is a calling. I began to hear that call again in 1989 in Boston.

My friend, patron and sometime student of art, Richard Clementi, had treated me to a movie. The movie was about teaching poetry to adolescents but an even deeper theme in the movie was the crisis teaching was in, a movement that I had encountered in graduate school as well as in practical applications. We were having coffee afterwards and I simply could not help myself. I began to cry.

Richard was a very sensitive man and quietly asked me what was wrong. I told him I was deeply moved by the movie and realized that I missed teaching. I decided right then to move back home to California and return to teaching. Was this my fateful error? How could that be in a nation that touts education as the key to its foundations in freedom? While practicing this road to freedom I encounter entrapment, ensnarled in betrayal deep within our very system.

Here were my three reasons that I found could be possibilities for me becoming a target. A target selected by a sinister mentality that is life threatening and capable of stripping away every idea held dear that builds a life worth living in the free world. In the final analysis, a terrorizing spirit that is unholy and that wants to invade every particle of being that is cherished and joyful was the enemy that aimed its hideous psychological and spiritual weapons at me with uncanny accuracy.

I was working in business in Boston in the late 1980's and putting together a major body of work in painting that was winning awards in international exhibits in New York. The work was defined by techniques of thick and thin acrylic paints and often metallic powders giving an illuminated effect emblazoned in the paintings. It was exhilarating to be painting and to gain recognition that I never thought possible. A whole segment of my work was dedicated to the effects of the nuclear holocaust called the winter white series. I hung a show in Harvard Square at a coffeehouse with this work. I was really experiencing the typical processes of creative thinking, painting, and exhibiting.

My daughter, Christina, came for a visit in the summer of 1988. I wanted her to think about going to college back east or working there. We both were aware of threatened species, possible extinction and especially the whales. The gray whale was extinct in the Atlantic because of whaling practices. I felt haunted by this and we decided to go on a whale watch in the Atlantic, sailing out of Boston Harbor on a scientific boat that the New England Aquarium operates and sails for local people and tourists. A marine biologist was our guide and he shared his wonderful knowledge of the history of whaling and its effects on marine biology. He identified a huge school of pilot whales that accompanied us out to sea swimming swiftly just under the surface of the water and surrounding the boat.

Our moods were upbeat and I was sketching away while my beautiful daughter enjoyed the voyage. We were well out to sea when I experienced something that changed my whole outlook and eventually my focus in art.

I was looking out as far as the eye could see on a deep horizon of blue when gray clouds tunneled around my sight. The sky was a brilliant sun-drenched blue. I was startled at first but I could not break away from the riveting magnetism on my gaze. My eyes fixed at the horizon line and the two colors of blue of sky and sea. I was very aware that I was not in control of my view. Then the sea turned choppy and the waves broke into lines and then in an instant the water was gone, and what was suspended beneath the sky in front of me was cracked earth, parched beyond belief. I knew God was present. He wanted me to see this vision and feel His sadness of the end of the ocean of life.

I felt my heart blend into His and knew the meaning of extinction. He told me to remember what I saw. Then it was gone and the shimmering waves animated the plane of water and brought me back to the edge of the boat as it sped along farther out into the Atlantic Ocean.

The guide's amplified voice cut through the air, excited by a humpback whale that came up to the edge of the boat with his baleen wide open and the ocean and its life pouring out the sides. We could almost touch him. Then he flipped and dove splashing and waving his tail at us as if he wanted us to follow him and play. I knew he was checking us out as he escorted our boat to a spectacular event.

We came to a quiet part like a calm sea within the ocean. Here were two other tiny boats bobbing around with dots of bright colors indicating the people on board who were watching like us. The sun was gleaming and the guide announced we were at a feeding ground for the humpbacks. If we watched the gulls flocking around we would soon see a whale breech the surface. There were probably ten flocks at every angle we looked. Also he advised us to look for a small rainbow over the surface and we would see the whales blowing. I called them rainbow blows because a little rainbow appeared as the waterspouts divided like prisms in the sunlight. We saw this wonderful picnic of probably twenty humpback whales feed and play. We stayed for almost an hour. I got plenty of sketches and witnessed the sheer joy of nature at its best entertain my daughter. Christina, who worried over dolphins in our cans of tuna during her grade school years, and the play of the whales, relaxed any harbored anxiety she might still have. Her face was full of grace and joy.

Then we headed back. I knew my "vision" had embedded in my mind and was working on my creative instincts into a major painting. After Christina left Boston I experienced a profound sadness. My sadness was accompanied by anxieties that forced me to finish the largest painting I have ever done and to think about my soul and my God. I did not know consciously then but I was beginning to dedicate my art talent to the Lord and working on putting my life in better order. My large painting titled "Venus Dying" was the start of my asking forgiveness for, most of all, my lack of faith and constant cynicism and my growing gratitude that we were living in a state of grace given by God. The body was submerged and breaking up into bright blue paint cracked with midnight blue brushstrokes in a stained glass effect. In the painting, the head was floating at the horizon in a large moon shape with ugly horns sprouting off the top. The face was "a woman in the moon" not a man. When I had finished my painting I thought I had painted the whore of Babylon and Jezebel and Venus all in one. I knew I did not want to become like her or a woman driven mad by revenge.

At this point I was virtually undisturbed by the people around me. I could stay busy at work and painting; competing in exhibits and take part in a New York show, which is the zenith for most people in the visual arts. It definitely was one of the highest points in my life. I had a compelling need to communicate through my artwork to whoever out there was looking. I tried writing but it was not working out so I put that away. But I wanted to communicate in poetry because language was growing lifeless for me. In a few months poetry would be my language.

I was in a three year holding pattern from the time of being discovered by a New York gallery, continuously receiving juried awards for exhibitions all which led up to the New York show and afterwards. The show officially opened up the New Year in 1989 but the reception would be a few days later. This was every serious artist's dream, to be discovered by a gallery in New York City, the art capitol of the world.

The gallery selected the works for the show. I was deeply touched by their selections. Out of 25 to 30 different paintings with three or four different themes and several techniques, they picked my "Angelharp", a painting of an angel floating over the hills and strumming a harp. It commemorated my daughter's choice on her sixteenth birthday for an angel's name to be her own and it was also my name. I wanted to celebrate with the joy of music that runs through my family so I added the harp. The first time I saw a harp or lyre was on my father's gravestone. It was a symbol of hope to me and here it was again. It was like Christina's first Christmas when she took her first steps on Christmas day, a gift to me. The other paintings were touching to me as well with the theme of music and musicians and a large mystical relational painting in a surreal theme of father and children. Christina lived far from me while she attended a private Christian school but I knew she had given a lot of thought and love to her life and to mine. I felt an immense amount of love between us and God and great respect.

At a later show in California, "Angelharp" was described by a show curator as naive. I smiled, she did not know I was in her tour group, and she did not know the painting had exhibited in New York City and had won several outstanding awards for excellence. I think she was experiencing what I went through, that people like what they like and the genuine surfaces to the top, and that is a surprise. For me it was a beautiful door opening up to the future and for the curator it was disappointment that art does not have to reflect the grim, weird or darkness of life. The painting was later selected to be shown in France in the International Grand Prix de Paris.

I was preparing to attend the show, my first opening in New York. I was feeling humble and decided to take the bus. The train from Boston to New York was standing room only. We wound through Harlem and then on to the bus station. I took a taxi to Greenwich Village. I walked around for a while and felt buoyed by the smiling faces and bustling crowds. I found a little restaurant and ordered a salad Nicoise. The atmosphere was gentle. After lunch I walked to the gallery that was in Soho. It was a bright, sunny but cold day. The gallery was in two different buildings and had several galleries. Mine was on the second floor. I climbed a long, steep flight of stairs to a gleaming white light filled gallery with three different areas for showing. I was pleased with how my paintings were hung. I had shipped the large one off the stretcher and it was professionally restretched. My paintings are best viewed in light directly on them because they have metallic powders on the surfaces of thick built up paint. Also there were bare areas to the linen, an enduring and deep influence I picked up from Toulouse Lautrec's work I had pored over at the Chicago Art Institute when I was a student. The work needed plenty of light in order to see the total effect they produced.

I left the gallery pleased. No one knew I was there. I wandered on looking for a drugstore because I needed some aspirin for the pain in my hip and lower back, which was aching from the cold weather. I had fallen down a flight of stairs in a loft where I had lived in Boston. It was where I was living when I received the letter of discovery from my gallery wanting to represent me. The incomparable elation I experienced at the news had kept me together after the fall and the pain along with moving to Southie where I had an apartment near the beach and my neighbors were in my own ethnic group, which was a new experience. All these factors lead up to this day, my first New York show. I was able to paint a substantial body of work for my portfolio while leading a somewhat peaceful life. After finding a pharmacy and making my purchase, I went to a nearby bar and grill just around the corner from the gallery for an early dinner.

Inside was a friendly barmaid so I sat down at the bar. She was in "New York time" and I learned a lot about her and New York within an hour. She was from Chicago and her friend next to me was, too. Her friend was visiting and learning about the city like me. It was my third time in the City but I had never seriously considered moving there until now. I invited them to my show, giving them invitations the gallery had provided with directions there. The barmaid was a psychology student at New York University and putting herself through school with her job. I told them about the startling and at the same time sweet selections from my work for the show and elaborated on their meanings. The barmaid told one horrifying story after another of life in the city. I had come to New York not only to attend the opening but also to check out the possibility of moving there in pursuit of my art career.

In my walk around Soho earlier I was looking for places to live. There were old buildings with brightly colorful banners waving from various heights, advertising galleries that were tucked into nooks and corners. But looking for a residential possibility took away the charm for me. It seemed very hard and industrial, not in the spirit the direction my work was taking. I had already had terrible experiences living in a warehouse loft space in Boston. It seemed like the atmosphere of Soho would multiply and intensify my negative living experiences. Living that romance was finished. The colorful banners flying in the city breeze, beckoning people to come in to the galleries was wonderfully exciting, like something I had never seen before. However, I sensed a violence underneath it all that was signaling me to think cautiously about this move. Now, listening to my new friends tell me about life as they were finding it filled in a lot of the negative gaps in my observations. It was a filthy place full of crime, a dark and dying hellhole living off former glamour and fame.

Then in a flash, two patrons went screaming and running after a blur of a figure, out the door to the sidewalk. I followed them with my eyes and was astonished to see it was dark outside. The show would open soon. All I could see was a human river of people. They returned in a few minutes, very upset, their voices loud and agitated spilling out that they had just been robbed of $500 in a hidden money belt. It was their entire vacation money. I shivered and pulled my own bag close to me. It was over within minutes and everything settled back down into the regular dinner hour.

The darkness had brought the violence close to me and I wanted to be at the reception where I felt comfortable and could greet guests as they arrived. Again I asked my two new friends to come to the opening, reminding them that the gallery was just around the corner. Then I left into the night. I scurried along with the crowd and it deposited me at the door of the gallery. I walked up the steep staircase again glad that my aspirin was working.

It was darker inside now and I anxiously climbed the last step to enter into a dimly lit room. I swallowed my breath and walked the gallery. Two brightly lit areas were all there were and unfortunately my paintings were in one of the dim areas. Next to me was the work of a Florida artist, full of color and brightness that was lost also, enveloped in the shadows. My heart sank. I walked back to the front to get a glass of wine and introduce myself to the wine steward/gallery receptionist. He knew everything that was going on so I knew I could ask him any questions. The gallery employees were all in wine colored uniform blazers with dark pants. They could be the consultants who sell our work, I had no idea but I was glad he was friendly. After some chitchat, I took my wine and went to the window seat to rest a while before the big crowds came. One of my new friends from Chicago that I met at the bar and grill arrived at the gallery. I guided her to the wine bar for a glass and then escorted her around the gallery for a tour. I mentioned my dismay about my paintings being in the dark. Maybe my work was positioned here because I was new in the gallery, this being my first show with them. I quit searching for answers when I noticed large groups of people beginning to fill up the gallery. My friend had to leave.

Shortly after she left, a crowd formed around one of the lighted areas next to mine and I noticed the artist was present, dancing between them and her work and talking to them. I was sorry my work was in a dimly lit area because it was wasted in the evening's opening. My consolation was that they shone in the brightness of daylight and that would help them sell. Also the artwork looked good in their slides for the gallery's presentations to clients around the city.

I was becoming tired and thinking about leaving when another group arrived swirling around a central figure, a lady dressed in black lace. Someone said something to her and she approached me. As she came forward, the surrounding crowd broke away. The wine steward was by my side introducing me to the gallery director, Nikki Santorini. I recognized her name on all the gallery correspondence to me. I was happy to meet her and held out my hand. She was there ahead of me and gave me a warm handshake and smile welcoming me. Her demeanor was so warmly genuine that all negative feelings were dispersed. Then the crowd swallowed her up as they moved along into the show.

They were in the second section with the dancing woman artist when I got up from my window seat to leave. I walked to the top of the flight of stairs. The elegant gentleman pouring the wine assured me a taxi would pick me up at the street. I looked down to the bottom of the stairs. There was a group of people preparing to climb. I noticed in the center was an elderly lady with her cane. Deciding to wait until they had reached the top before descending, my gaze focused on this dear lady who had come out into the violent night to climb this mountain of stairs in her pain to see the artwork including mine! She was dressed in sparkling evening attire and I was glad I had worn my midnight blue sequined beret that I had purchased especially for the opening. It was a perfect ending to a spectacular art opening and it was the New Year, 1989.

I watched her and her group be swallowed up into the gallery darkness and then turned to the stairs taking them one by one. I reached the bottom and rushed out into the night, into the street to a waiting cab. It was an exciting and informative 24 hours in New York on the pinnacle of my success as an emerging artist. On the dark bus ride home I quietly decided not to move to Soho or Greenwich Village. It was a remarkable place, a culture where kindergarten teachers collect artwork, thinking nothing of coming to the hidden galleries to shop. However, it was not about my lifestyle. I could sell my work there but I could not live there. Thirty-seven years earlier my father had made the same decision. He auditioned and was accepted into one of the most famous big bands in the U.S. But the habits and lifestyles of the band were too different from my father's. He turned the offer down and left New York for the West. I had been impressed by the gallery's choices of my work, no dark themes. Maybe I could sell there but live elsewhere.

After my show all the forces around me changed and I found myself funneling into a whirlwind. The movie and coffee with my friend Richard was the pivotal point in time that changed my entire physical location.

I was flying home to Monterey, California by summer within 24 hours of making the decision to move. My things, my life's work was stored in Boston until I could send for them. My mother, always sympathetic to my artistic endeavors sensed my need to relocate and wired me the money to fly home. When I arrived my mother announced that Christina was also moving to California to live here and attend college. I was elated.

Within two months, I had a California Teaching Credential and had been selected as a Professional Artist in the Schools. I was also doing some temporary office work. One of my jobs brought me to a small hotel in a plaza in one of the small towns that ringed the Monterey Bay. The concierge invited me to go to the coffeehouse next to where the hotel was located. There were live entertainment and poetry readings.

The first crushing blow was from Christina. She called to say she had changed her plans from moving to California to moving to Oregon. Jay, the boy who lived next door to us while they were in grade school, the boy on the trip to New York and points east when they were children, had called to ask her to come to Oregon. He was flying her there and paying for moving her things. There was nothing I could say. I had raised her to make her own decisions and now I had to live with them.

I began writing there in the coffeehouse and meeting artists, poets, musicians, and other teachers. Soon I was reading my poems at open readings sometimes accompanied by musicians. The entire energy force and atmosphere around me were buoyant as we moved along the politics of instituting the marine life sanctuary.

My love for my new home with all its spectacular beauty and friendly people was tempered by a drought. Drought occurs in this area almost regularly in cycles of seven years; seven years of rain then seven years of drought. It was several years into the drought when I arrived. I remembered my mother writing to me soon after she and my stepfather and sister moved from the rainy Pacific Northwest to Carmel Valley in the seventies. I could not comprehend what it meant until we went to visit them. They had buckets and tubs of "used" water in the bathtub in which to water plants and quickly bathe. I was then living in a climate that rained constantly for nine months of the year in Portland, Oregon.

Now I was living in another drought. We could take 3-minute showers because all property was given a legal limit of water usage. Landlords and hotel owners were being fined thousands of dollars for going over their allotted usage. In every public restroom were warning signs about running the water too long to simply wash your hands. It was the end of getting an automatic free glass of water at a restaurant. Water was on request and sometimes could cost up to a quarter a glass.

The drought was a leveler and affected everyone no matter how rich or poor. A friend took me to a nearby national forest. The park ranger at the entrance warned us about how extremely dry the timber was. We drove in and at the bottom of a wide canyon was a tiny trickle of green water. As we walked along twigs snapped and debris crunched. It was like walking into a hell waiting to be lit. I later wrote the following poem about the experience.

Landing in the Canyon
(Arroyo Seca Canyon in Los Padres National Forest, California)

It was one of those finite days
perspective disappeared at dawn,
there was no place left to be alive
except traveling.
We were.

The sky contained a cloudbank
with shreds of fog laying across
the mountains, the valley was clear

and empty of traffic,
except a few swans
flying close to earth.

Turning we faced
a guard fog bank protecting
a mountain wizard,
ominous in depth and height.
I knew we could pass
the ambivalence lurking
in the thick of it.

The sun sparkled on and
we were welcomed into the
mountains.

It was a deep canyon
we confronted.
At the bottom, a ribbon of
green water
cooly eyed us as we approached.
The yellow surface opened up
providing a place
at last
where we could land.

Descent was spectacular.
I knew we would not fall,
the atmosphere was buoyant
yet deep enough
to attract our attention
for hours of landing
until we were

breathing over the
rocky terrain.

A bed of sand unfolded
softly…
and peacefully
we brushed the earth,
unwinding our bodies
into the kindness
of its polished grains,
warmed by the sun.
The air cooled by the
canyon river greeting us
beside our weary bodies.

Our skins were refreshed
and comforted
as we landed in
the canyon.

This was how life was in what some people call a paradise. Little did I know that there were people near me who would hurt me and try to destroy the meaning of all the hard work and the mastery of God. Often in the midst of it all, I would repeat a little phrase to God, "I'm here, I'm alive." I was hoping to feel His presence again like on the whale watch boat in the Atlantic. I was beginning to feel lost, my work was on the east coast and I wanted to re-connect with it. I had turned down a contract renewal with my gallery in New York that turned out to be a wise decision because the entire New York art scene went into a collapse. Some of my new paintings were reflecting my feelings of abandonment, growing more and more abstract. However, a new perspective on life was taking over my creative side. Its theme was the beauty of life. I wanted to live it just like I wanted to speak in poetry. Beauty is kindness and sacred.

I was living in the quiet little town where the plaza was that housed the coffee-house I patronized and where most of my new friends lived. I often took long walks along the path by the oceanfront. It was peaceful for me. I felt close to my

Creator here. It was a place where even butterflies could be protected. One day towards the end of the day I was walking along and wanted to take the steps down to a little beach when several of the butterflies flew into my face. I was tired and it was annoying. I wanted to rest a while on the beach but every step I took towards my goal more butterflies would fly at me. I decided not to argue with them and walked home. I lay down on my bed and all of sudden the whole earth was shaking. I was the only one at home. I stood up gripping the windowsill to look outside. A cat was below my window crouched flat down to the ground. When the shaking stopped in a matter of seconds; off ran the cat. I ran out the door to see many neighbors in the street. It was an earthquake. I thought it was ironic that in the early part of the decade (the 80's) I had left California because of the big earthquake warning and Christina had gone to live with her dad and his new family. The house was not damaged but electrical and phone lines were out for the next three days.

I have often thought back to the beautiful butterflies that chased me away from the dangerous rocks of the beach. A few towns up the coast part of the cliffs collapsed killing a man on the beach.

3

The Approach

o o o o o o o o o o o o o o o o o o o o o o o o o o o o o o o o o o o o
"Do not be overcome by evil but overcome evil with good."

—*Romans 12:21*

The Monterey Peninsula has a series of small towns strung together along the coastline. A friend of mine once said, "You pay rent for a spectacular view." Housing was expensive and salaries were small but there was always the view of the Bay if not from your residence, then just a few steps ahead. The ambience was high with an invasive value.

In the fall of 1990 I was living in a tiny duplex with two other women roommates, Joanie and Trish. We felt fortunate to get this place that was affordable plus had a large concrete work space outside that would serve perfectly for me as a painting area.

We were able to move in because one of the women knew the lady in the other side of the duplex. Her name was Judi and she was in theater, performing in local productions occasionally. She was a student at the local community college.

One night Judi and I were talking and she said she knew someone that I should meet. His name was Hanafi and he was really sweet and generous and that he worked at the local community college that she attended. We walked a few blocks to his apartment. He was not home but his car was there. I told Judi I really was not that interested but she wrote a note and left it on his car windshield anyway stating that we had been there. Then we walked back home. I asked her about Hanafi's name, what did it mean? She mumbled something but I did hear her say it was Muslim. I thought over my experiences with the Muslim faith and its people and the Islamic culture. I had taught Muslim children in a parochial school way back in the 1970's. They were exemplary students. My graduate school was largely funded by an oil rich Middle Eastern country due to the enrollment of one of the royal family's princes. I had some knowledge about what being a Muslim meant since I had taken a graduate level class on their culture. However, I was ill prepared for what was to come.

When I got back, Joanie was talking about repainting the apartment. I agreed that it would brighten everything up and improve lifestyle. The weekend was coming up and it would be a good time to start. I called Christina and she sounded busy. I thought everything sounded ok between her and Jay. She had a job and was trying for a better one already.

That fateful Friday evening I was pleasantly tired and glad to be home. We were all sitting around talking. I was sitting on the floor drinking a beer thinking to myself that I had turned my life around and made a decision to stay socially unavailable to dating. I had two failed marriages and ten years of sporadic dating and a couple of shallow relationships behind me. But my attitude towards being in a love relationship or marriage had evaporated or soured, I wasn't sure. My door was closed.

Suddenly, lights flashed in the windows and a car crept up slowly in the driveway, crunching the gravel and evaporating my pleasant, pensive mood. I could sense the other women tensing up and Trish jumped up with a look of startled expectation. She ran to the door and looked through the curtained window. She whirled around and in a frightened voice blurted out, "Hanafi's here!" Joanie uttered a low laugh of disbelief and I was in a nervous state of vigilance, edgy at the thought of a stranger intruding on a quiet night. There was no excitement coming from these two that meant a nice man was coming over to visit. No, they were both scared.

In a panic they stood up and sat down several times chattering between themselves about what this event might mean. I said we should just stay calm and discourage him from staying. We all agreed on that and then his knock came on the door.

Trish let him in and he sat down immediately. His visage was enshrouded by a dark shadow preventing me from seeing him very clearly. He began to speak and his voice, contrary to his arrival, was calm. He wanted to see our apartment and had heard we wanted to paint it. I thought of Judi but any thinking dissolved when his language changed into a lurid suggestion to first Joanie then Trish whom both put him in his place. He skipped me probably because he did not know who I was. Later when I reflected back to this incident I realized that both of the women had some knowledge of character and that this man was not the sweet, generous person Judi had spoken about. Fear was blurring my mind and fear was rising inside me when he spoke again somewhat indicating this next part he was talking about was for me.

He said he would paint our apartment for us if we would help him. He was moving out of his apartment into a studio in a couple of weeks. We all looked at each other with surprise when he asked us to go with him to his new place. I could tell Trish was interested because it meant less work. Trish and I piled into his car and drove with him to his new place.

It looked like a small compound, with a warehouse behind a little house that rented to a couple of commercial businesses. Next door was a small house used as a residence. He unlocked the door for us. Trish was completely turned off by the warehouse studio idea but I had seen this set-up before for artists as work and live studios back east. A large room with a crudely built bathroom and a tiny kitchen in one corner was the layout. Industrial type windows covered one wall. There was a door that opened into an identical space but with no living improvements. It was used as storage for restaurant equipment.

Trish stood in the living area of the studio like a wild deer caught in traffic, her big eyes growing bigger while they surveyed everything. I was sure she did not want to ever come back let alone help him with the work of moving in and fixing the space up to a living standard. She did not speak but walked out and went home. I think I would have preferred that she scream, and then I would dash out too.

There I was alone with this strange man. He was quick to speak after we noticed Trish had left. He said we could get his work done in a couple of weekends and then he would paint our apartment for us. He said it would only take a couple of days. He backed up his offer with the fact that he was a handyman on the weekends and was used to doing this work.

All my fears of this man left for some reason as soon as Trish was gone and I did not know why. He smiled and started to tell me he wanted me to teach him how to paint and that he wanted to be my friend. Little did I know what that would mean to me in the next few months and how it would change my life.

4

The Lure

"All mortals are but a breath,
  Mere phantoms, we go our way;
      mere vapor, our restless pursuits;
      we heap up stores without knowing
        for whom."

—Psalm 39:7

It was the middle of October and I was the only one who was working on our bargain. I spent about two weeks with Hanafi as we fixed up his studio and then moved his belongings over to his studio. He impressed me with his industriousness and quickness.

During this time he proceeded to tell me a little about himself. In my mind I took it all in as the truth simply on the fact that he was accepted into the community in his employment and his relationship with his landlord.

He said he was really interested in keeping part of the studio for art. He wanted me to teach him how to paint because he had a sincere interest in it. He suggested the possibility of converting the space next door into a working studio for me. All he had to do was convince the landlord who had an office on the premises in the little house that was in front of the warehouse and he would do the work. Then I would be all set. I could move my belongings from back east and go into production again. My sketchbook was full of ideas and I was excited that everything could work out this well.

He seemed like a haunted man to me and when he told me he was trying to escape from a group of people that scared him I understood the look. He said they had quit bothering him lately and he wanted to be totally free of them. He said it was something like a religious cult and they try to tell him what to do. Sometimes he would shudder when he thought of them. He said he had no personal life with them.

I really perked up with this information. Some of my graduate training involved discerning cults and analyzing them by breaking down their premises or more likely promises that are used to manipulate members. I wanted to learn more of this group, who they were, where they were and what they were. I was working.

We worked continually and then after we moved him in we had a mini party, just the two of us. He had earned my trust. The attention he showered on me filled a lonely gap in my life since my second marriage had ended nearly ten years ago.

Then he came over to our place and painted it all in one weekend. Even Joanie and Trish were impressed. He had cleaned up his language with me and was polite to all of us, often making us laugh with jokes and stories. He did such a professional job and made us all feel good about who he was. Judi's words seemed to ring true. We were particularly proud of our apartment when he was finished because it was so clean and pleasant. Judi had let hers go and in fact had not been around much, like she had lost interest in her life there.

I began staying at Hanafi's more and more. He was fun and entertaining and generous. Underneath the growing relationship was my eye on the place next door as a future studio.

He had not said much about the group that was bothering him and our conversations had turned away from anything dark and foreboding.

One night we were in his studio when he asked me to move in with him. I protested that I had a place close by but he said he had more room. I gave in and he said triumphantly, "Let's get your stuff now!" I thought he was kidding. It was nighttime and I was tired. It was as if he had unending energy.

We drove over to the apartment and packed up my things and moved them out to the consternation of my roommates. However, I told them they would have more room now without me. Besides, I had heard that Judi was moving and she was our ticket with our landlord. A new management company had taken over the duplex and I had a feeling that things were going to change. It was Halloween eve.

From the car I saw Joanie and Trish run out the door, their arms outreached towards me. They were crying to me not to leave. I watched them through the car window, tears in my eyes; my heart was breaking at my own folly. I had no personal power. I had no choices. This man, this situation, overwhelmed me. I felt horribly alone. It was Halloween and the car pulled out of the driveway at midnight with all my possessions and me.

In a few days I found out Joanie and Trish would have to leave the duplex because the new management that had taken over was raising the rent beyond their limits. Even if I had stayed, there would not have been enough money.

5

The Story

o o o o o o o o o o o o o o o o o o o o o o o o o o o o o o o o o

"If you make the Most High your
        Dwelling
            even the LORD, who is my refuge
Then no harm will befall you,
            no disaster will come near your
                tent.
For he will command his angels
                concerning you
            to guard you in all your ways;
They will lift you up in their hands,
            so that you will not strike your foot
                against a stone.
You shall tread upon the lion and the
                cobra;
            you will trample the great lion and
                the dragon.

"Because he loves me," says the Lord,
            "I will rescue him;
        I will protect him, for he
            acknowledges my name."

—Psalm 91:9-14

The next few days were spent unpacking, repacking my things. The smallness of the studio facilitated only useful items. All my art supplies, small paintings, and writings were repacked and the boxes stored in a corner. Somewhere in the back of my mind I noted that these were my daily useful things but I compromised and put them away wondering when I would get back to my creative activities. They were like life to me.

November was bright and beautiful. The "plein air" atmosphere the local impressionists relish on Monterey Bay Peninsula coast extended into the Indian summer. Hanafi was busy seven days a week working at the local community college as an employment counselor and on weekends painted new houses in the richest part of the area. I held a huge yard sale for him in front of the warehouse and we made over $200. I was working evenings in a local stock brokerage as the night manager for a telemarketing crew. Hanafi introduced me to the landlord whose office was in the little house in front of the studio. He said that "the ole' man" had been in the navy and was quite rich. Hanafi often did work for him on his properties. Everything seemed fine and I felt accepted.

In the evenings when everything calmed down, he would sit in his chair and tell me parts of his life's story.

He had a rough upbringing in a large family. They subsisted as migrant workers in the fields and orchards up and down the coast. Originally he came from the Seattle area and his family was of German descent, specifically the nobility. His father had left the family when he was in high school, a hopeless alcoholic. He said it really got rough with just his mom for support. They were Roman Catholics but he said the Church never really helped them. In later days he caught up with his dad and found him working for the Salvation Army. He died after making peace with his son over a poker game. His mother was in a nursing home in the Modesto area but he never visits her. This was the only time he made a reference to anything Christian and it was with sour distaste and prejudicial.

He still had family, he said, up in the Modesto area and they were planning a big party for Thanksgiving and he wanted to bring me to meet everyone. We would stay over night returning on the Friday after Thanksgiving.

I was in a positive anticipatory mood but a little anxious at the whirlwind pace of everything. I got my hair cut and highlighted and bought a new outfit in November yellows with lots of brown lace trim, accented with gold studs.

Our evening chats continued and he told me he had been married three times and had children by two of his wives. His children were gone from the area. I noticed a picture of one, a little girl, on a bookshelf and assumed it was his daughter, although she held no resemblance at all to him.

He also was trying to tell me about the "group" from which he was trying to break. His voice was anxious when he said one of the members had called him recently and was pressuring him to return to them. He said they have a lot of power. He said they were of the Muslim faith and I was surprised because he drank alcohol every evening with ease. For the first time Hanafi named them. He called them the Shubus.

Thanksgiving was quick in arriving. We packed up the car and left for a much needed holiday. I had never been to the Modesto area. It was agricultural with miles of almond, walnut, and apricot trees. His "family" was all there in a tidy house. Couples and singles and us, no children were there. When we arrived we were warmly greeted. Someone put a beer in my hand and introductions were made but the names and faces blurred for me. Everyone seemed genuinely happy to meet me. I knew he had talked to them about me before we arrived.

Besides the heavy drinking, I was struck by one odd fact that no one looked like Hanafi. He was dark, swarthy and short. Everyone was fair-skinned, blond and tall.

It turned out to be a pleasant holiday with lots of teasing going on among "family members". On the way back home he wanted to stop at his son's house outside of San Jose. His son lived in a mobile home with his pretty wife and darling little girl. They were very busy with her family and their business. Hanafi enjoyed being with his grandchild and visiting. He was very affectionate towards them. I was struck again at how no one had his features. They were all fair-skinned and blond.

We left after a couple of hours and I was very relaxed. As we got closer to home, I suggested we stop and meet my family as a surprise. My mother does not celebrate Thanksgiving at home anymore preferring instead to go out to dinner. However, she welcomed us in when we arrived. Hanafi brought a six-pack in with him and asked if anyone wanted one. No one was accustomed to this gesture in my family. My brother-in-law was there and took a beer, trying to size him up, wondering what in the world he was doing with me. I told everyone who Hanafi was and his position at the college and that he was a Muslim but that he was leaving that faith. My mother must have registered this fact because in a week we had our Christmas presents from her. They were two woolen Christmas stockings with our names written in gold. It was such a surprise to me because I considered her to be spiritually confused or void. I would later realize that she was sending him a powerful message. The message was no matter what we may seem like we are Christians. Later on I was grateful for this small gesture because it perhaps saved my life.

The next few weeks were spent in nightly outpourings of Hanafi's past. He wanted me to know about him. He made a big deal about his horoscope which was Capricorn and that we were in a special month that was full of fire, December. He was trying to get me to relate to him through our sun signs. He did not understand that I was putting such things out of my life. I was really surprised at how insistent he was about the astrology since he had been a devout Muslim or so he said. I had studied that faith in art history classes in graduate school and had talked with newly immigrated Muslims from Egypt. One thing they made clear was that alcohol was forbidden and I never saw or heard any references to astrology. Was this part of his escape? I did not know.

As December weeks sped by towards Christmas, I had pieced together quite a story from him. The Muslim group that Hanafi belonged to began somewhere in Indonesia under the guidance of a very wonderful and sacred man. The man had passed away but his teachings were in the slim red book Hanafi kept on the bed stand. He kept pointing to it but I was not that interested yet. I knew it was not the holy book of Islam, the *Koran*. He said the original group in Indonesia was full of the master's goodness and they were very spiritual. But he said that the group here wasn't like that and that he was afraid of them. I kept asking myself, "What were they going to do?" and "Where were they?" Drinking, astrology—maybe these were his defense mechanisms for deprogramming. I did not know how to help him but I could listen. It seemed to be what he needed and I was growing more interested in terms of what this group meant for our community.

My graduate school training was taking over which had included the study of false prophets and cults and how they eclipse lives, brainwashing, and controlling until the respondents are broken down and act on the leader's cues or commands. I had not learned any deprogramming techniques except avoidance. I was slipping slowly into a murky existence I had never known before. The nightly talks were turning towards the darkness of life. However, I remained an apt listener if for no other reason to find a way out because I was trapped.

6

The Eve of War

o o o o o o o o o o o o o o o o o o o o o o o o o o o o o o o o o

"The stars of heaven and their
constellations
will not show their light;
The rising sun will be darkened
and the moon will not give its
Light."

—*Isaiah 13:10*

Christmas was near and Hanafi's drinking was increasing if that was possible. He agreed to get a little live decorated tree from the supermarket. So we had our stockings and our tree with a few gifts. The tv was on most of the time, something I was not used to but it was cable tv and it was comforting to me. He was gone often in the evenings which made me grateful having never a seen a full-blown alcoholic before.

He told me about losing custody of his daughter, which broke his heart. They were very close. He described the relationship like playmates. When one of her friends' mother turned him in to authorities as an unfit father he lost the suit in court and lost custody of his daughter then. He called her almost every other evening during the holidays talking about when they could get back together. I was beginning to be in the way. His voice was beginning to change into a whine and sounding like a little boy. I knew the girl was out of the state with relatives but I felt sorry for her because he was pressuring her so much.

Christmas came and went rather uneventfully. I got a beautiful glass Christmas platter from a lady who drew my name at work. Hanafi got a large painted wood nutcracker, the kind that was in "The Nutcracker Suite". My Christmas spirit was challenged and I was glad when the holiday was over. I noted consciously that anything having to do with Christmas did not offend him. I took it as a sign that he was safe from the feared organization that was after him, the Shubus.

I called Christina and she announced her engagement to Jay on the phone. I was happy for her. Jay got on the phone and told me he had hidden her ring in a box of laundry soap and laughed. I laughed too but I did not know why. I have never understood why he did that but it seemed insulting to me. The tinge of negativism was beginning to coat everything.

Hanafi came home one night after Christmas and announced that we had been invited back to his "family" in Modesto for a New Year's Eve party. It was going to be really special because we were going to camp out at a lake and New Year's Day, everyone was going to water ski in wetsuits. I could not imagine this happening and protested that I was not well and did not want to go. He insisted I go with him. Little did I know what was ahead.

Hanafi was growing excited to leave for the party with every day. He said the most exciting part was the blue moon would be out on New Year's Eve. I asked him what that meant thinking it would be wonderful just to stay warm at home. He said it marks a special time and astrologically it was real important because "a blue moon" only occurs once in a while.

We packed and left on New Year's Eve day. It was very cold and I was not looking forward to the experience. We all met at a little lake where some people already had their tents set up. There were several bonfires lit even though it was only late afternoon. A tent was set up for us near the bonfire. There were chairs around the fire and I immediately sat in one not willing to give up my warmth.

The men kept the fire going from late afternoon clear into the night past midnight. Of course everyone there was already drinking. I was not comfortable and felt uneasy. As midnight approached, the blue moon rose over the lake. Someone tried to point out to me the color of it but it looked like an ordinary moon to me. It was all very important but to me it was very meaningless and foolhardy.

I was sitting by the fire and Hanafi was by my side being very congenial when all of a sudden the man I knew as his brother-in-law appeared out of the dark. His fist came crashing down into Hanafi's face as he cried out. I jumped up and away it was so close I thought he would hit me next. It was over as quickly as it began and Hanafi fled to the tent in pain like a wounded animal. I went over to him to see if he needed any help but he pushed me away. I climbed into my sleeping bag to get warm now that the bonfire area was unsafe. I slept off and on afraid that something more might happen. The blue moon was evil to me, a sign of bone-chilling cold and violence.

The next morning was bright, clear, and colder than the day before. People were taking down their tents and gathering at the small beach by the lake. I realized there were lots of people, more than from the night before. Men had on wetsuits and there were several boats at the dock. We broke camp and walked over to watch. I was coughing and sick from being in the cold all night. I watched through my pain as men water-skied around the lake. I was numb inside and out and wanted to go home.

Soon it was over, some ritual of pain I failed to understand. Hanafi's eye was blackening and I was glad when he said we could go home. He was silent the whole way.

When we arrived, his eye was swollen almost shut and the area around it was a deep black with broken blood vessels spidering in a circle around it. He did not want any help preferring to look after it himself.

During the next few days he wanted to tell me more about himself. He kept the lights low as he unfolded more of his story.

He told me his real name was Kenneth Feist and people called him Kenny. However, when he became a Muslim he changed it to Hanafi. He met the people in the organization when he was homeless and sleeping in his car. A group of these "devotees" approached him and convinced him to join them. In order to prove himself worthy he was to commit a federal offense, become a felon. He found the opportunity by stealing a credit card and going on an interstate shopping spree. He was caught and spent two years in a federal prison back east. He often had aliases but he said it was worth it because he was initiated into the group. He belonged.

He married a woman in the group and they were living out in the country in a trailer. One night he built a big bonfire and danced around it for hours. After a while a spirit joined him. The spirit was Hanafi. It was an angel sent from Allah. He welcomed him and took his name as his own. His name meant angel. I looked at him with his deep black eye and thought Hanafi is an angel, an angel from hell!

Later, I wrote a poem about Kenny's transformation into Hanafi.

An Angel Named Hanafi

I sat down one
evening,
and had a quiet talk
(mostly I just listened,
if you ask the right question,
you can do that)
with an angel and a man
named
Hanafi.

They both had a
conversation
high on a mountain,
by a blazing fire,
analyzing their lives,
one at the other.

Away walked the man,
his name became
like the angel's
Hanafi,
as he tried to convince me
he was just an

old cowboy angel
from Arabia.

But I knew
he was really an
demon from Hell.

He said his marriage broke up but he got custody of his daughter and he took her to live with him on the Monterey Peninsula. They lived together for several years until the girl's friend's mother pressed charges and he lost custody. He spoke about his time with his daughter with longing and it seemed almost like a lost love. Then he said the charges were dismissed in court and in order to protect her, he sent her away to her aunt's home out of state. He was trying to convince me it was ok. How else could he continue to live and work in the area if it wasn't? The group kept him for a while then he tried to break away because they had too much control over his life.

I was growing suspicious of him and was trying to scrape together enough money to move out. But I was terribly sick with pneumonia and couldn't work. Hanafi would bring home vitamins for me and let me just sleep during the day. I thought this was kind of him, but I was delirious with fever as well. The news on television was about Iraq's invasion of Kuwait.

7

The Demon

o o o o o o o o o o o o o o o o o o o o o o o o o o o o o o o o o
"Put on the full armor of God so that you can take your stand
against the devil's schemes."

—Ephesians 6:11

The Gulf war acted like a cue to Hanafi. He displayed an instant personality
change and any kind of tranquility at home was demolished by his transformation, which was the very day the war was announced.

His rudeness was unmatched by what I was to watch a steep descent into per-
version and madness. He told me what was happening. It was called "The jihad".
I couldn't understand him and I had never heard of the word. I asked him to
explain. He said we were in "the call of the jihad, the call of the 20 nations". He
was drooling at the mouth by now as he spoke, his whining voice reaching a
piercing shrillness. Triumphantly he beamed, "This is what we've been waiting
for!" I didn't want to talk too much longer because I was shocked and speechless
at this spectacle. I managed to ask him what that meant. He said, "The call of the
jihad was a holy war to bring to the end the state of Israel. The end of Israel." He
was delirious. I had never heard of this in any of my art history studies of Islamic
culture. His words were ugly and left me afraid. His eyes were gleaming and confident of victory. We watched the special reports and he drank himself into obliv-
ion. I was relieved that he had passed out. I was sleeping on the floor. The fever
had broken and the pneumonia was diminishing. I knew I would not be able to
live here much longer.

The next day I went to one of the coffeehouses where I read poetry. I sat down
at the bar. The tv was on and there was only news about the war. I talked with

the owner for a while and with a few other customers. The war was the only topic of conversation and we all agreed that Iraq had to be stopped, that it was crazy what was happening. The surprise of a Muslim nation attacking another Muslim nation was wearing off. In the back of my mind I thought how unusual for Christian nations to fight for a Muslim nation, but I never spoke about it.

For weeks, Hanafi would come home in an ugly mood. Sometimes he threw dishes breaking them against a wall, other times he would dance around drunk out of his mind, babbling to himself. I withstood a month of this deviant behavior with no end in sight because I didn't have enough money saved up yet to move.

One day I was watching the news alone on tv and a message flashed on the screen stating if anyone had any information concerning terrorists or attacks on U.S. citizens to call the FBI immediately. I knew Hanafi would be gone all day so I flew to the phone. I thought there was no office in Monterey at that time so I looked in the Santa Cruz phone directory and there was a number. I dialed not thinking it would register on the phone bill later. My idea was to call and then make plans to vacate the premises.

The agent on the other end was very calm but intently interested in what I was saying. I could hear my own voice elevate into a scream, a scream of terror, as I related how Hanafi's behavior had changed overnight with the news of the war. I told him about his wanting to get out of a cult group but it seemed like they had gotten to him. I told him about the "jihad" mispronouncing it. I could hear the agent stumble with the word too, the strangeness its sound and the meaning not known yet. He said he had never heard of this idea before. I told him I wanted to leave because I was so afraid of the situation. I let him know that I had investigated cult groups before especially one that had tried to invade my daughter's school community. I told him there was a book somewhere in the studio and also a list of local members. He asked me if I could stay for a while longer to get more information. Without thinking I said yes. He said he was contacting the San Francisco office for orders and that he would get back to me. I thought it would be easy and then I could clear out and be safe again.

I rummaged around the studio and found the cult list. I went out and made a copy of it, coming right back to put it in its place so Hanafi wouldn't suspect anything. One of the principles from which I had taught art was observation and

I had pushed it to life saving grace. I felt a fullness like a protective coating flow over me. I believe now this was a shield from God to protect me from what was to come.

Hanafi came home later than usual that evening. I was thankful for any time without him around. He went into the bathroom and was there for about 30 minutes. I was sitting out in the studio in front of the tv. The colors in the room changed sharply like the atmosphere was charged with some hot electrical current. The bizarre combinations robbed the objects in the room of their meanings. I saw his shadow and then he moved to stand half behind the bathroom door and halfway in my view. I summoned the courage to watch. He was displaying all kinds of deviate sexual perversions that were beyond my vocabulary. He was in slow motion and the display seemed to last an hour but I'm sure it was only a few minutes. Then he dashed outside to show the neighbors. He had a crimson robe on and stood there exposed and yelling at the top of his lungs for about 15 minutes. Somebody yelled at him and his spell was broken. He came in crying like a little boy, a bad little boy. He was shouting "People of the jihad will commit murder for Allah! If they do so they will go straight to Allah in his heaven. It is a blessing!" Then he drank himself to sleep waking up once because he wet his bed.

The next day as soon as he was gone I called the Santa Cruz FBI office again to tell them I found the list. There were probably thirty names with addresses and phone numbers. He said, "Good work!" Then I said I wanted to leave as soon as possible. He said I should get out now. I knew I couldn't leave everything behind, not again. All my writings, my art supplies and miniatures, no I couldn't do that. I felt so lost.

I sat down drained by this ugly encounter. I turned to God and prayed for a sign. A sign to show me He was near. I prayed for rain. It was the first time I realized that I had never seen Hanafi pray or even talk about prayer.

8

The Rain Prayer

o o o o o o o o o o o o o o o o o o o o o o o o o o o o o o o o o
"I am the Alpha and the Omega, the Beginning and the End. To him who is thirsty I will give to drink without cost from the spring of the water of life."

—Revelations 21:6

It was February and cold for California. Hanafi came in from work plastered and his mood was malignant. He started screaming, throwing a tantrum. He slapped me and yelled that he wanted me to get out now. I told him I was arranging to move my things to storage and would leave in a few days. He was weaving all over the studio, screaming and yelling for me to leave. Then he started to move my things outside. He put a tarp over them and came back in and told me to go. I told him I was calling the police. I picked up the phone, dialed the number and as I was speaking to the dispatcher, Hanafi lunged at me. But he was so drunk he missed and I was able to give the address before he grabbed the phone and slammed it down breaking the lifesaving connection. The police arrived in five minutes, a long five minutes for me as I dodged him around the studio.

There was a policeman at the door and two at the back of the patio area where my things were. They had their hands on their guns. As I explained to the officer the situation, Hanafi would interrupt with outbursts of protests that he wanted me out. The police wanted me to leave with them then but I didn't understand. I was still very civilized about matters and wanted to move all my things out tomorrow.

All of a sudden Hanafi went through one of his transformations and became very cooperative. It was a sudden personality switch back to a more reasonable state of mind. He was like the kind and generous Hanafi, the one that opened the doors for him in life, the Hanafi Judi had first told me about months ago.

I was amazed at how quickly he could perform these transformations. He told the officer I could stay the night and that he would take care of everything tomorrow. He would get me a mailbox at the post office, get a storage area and move my things into it. The bill for the storage would be sent to my post office box. But I had to leave tomorrow. I agreed. The police were satisfied and so was Hanafi.

The door closed. I didn't want to talk to him or listen to him. I just wanted to get to sleep. He continued to drink and menace around me, screeching and cackling, then whining like he was hurt. He was a creature, a demon, and I was in his territory. He wouldn't let go until he passed out. Then he would wake up again for another hour of hell. All the time the atmosphere in the room was charged with an unearthly color of red. Finally he passed out for the night. I sat in a corner all night, holding myself shivering but too afraid to go to sleep.

Light broke through the windows and I was out the door, never to return again. I found a room in a house in the town where most of my friends lived. I was free and the Gulf War was over.

As soon as I was settled I called the San Francisco FBI office to let them know where I was. I had rented a furnished room with a bath in a quiet neighborhood back in the town where I had started my poetry readings. I came and went for about a month. I had very little money only eating once a day and that was meager, a boiled egg, an orange, and a bagel. I was lean and learning the meaning of food as fuel.

I telephoned my daughter at Jay's house to find another shock. Christina had moved out. They gave me a phone number. I hung up quickly and called her. I was overjoyed to hear her voice at the other end. Then she told me she and Jay had broken up and she had moved on. I let out a spontaneous shout. I was heartbroken. She sounded great and had landed the job she was going for that she had mentioned the last time we had talked. I told her I was ok. We chatted for a while and then hung up. I was stinging from the news. But I didn't feel badly. I had just been through a horrific life-threatening experience and no one in Jay's family cared. They were trying to get Christina to marry him quickly, Jay's mother offering her the wedding gown from her wedding. Nothing had seemed right about the engagement. Slowly the stinging was subsiding, I knew she was safe and well and moving up in the world. She knew a little about what had happened to me but I really wanted to protect her from too much knowledge about the terrorists since the world wasn't ready for it either. It didn't make the news.

One day I was sitting around with friends at one of our gathering places, drinking coffee, watching chess players and greeting friends as they came and went. Boldly I mentioned the name of this cult group asking if anyone had heard of it. Immediately another gentleman in one of the games spoke up. "Why yes," he was chuckling, "they're just a group of laid back folk that get together to have a few laughs."

I said, "No, they're not." My voice was deep and quiet. I went on explaining that they were a group dedicated to a mission called a jihad or holy war and were part of a worldwide network of terrorism. They believed they were sanctioned by Allah incorporating terrorists' ideas and that their goal is the destruction of Israel. They could commit murder if necessary or give their lives and Allah would reward them generously in his heaven. I was afraid to mention anything about Christianity.

I was trying to keep my voice calm and hoping that my eyes were steady. The man spoke again and said that he doubted if they meant any harm. I grew quiet again. It disturbed me to listen to his dismissal of the meaning I had come to know. My mind was blocking out most of the recent events probably for protection. But one realization managed to surface and that was that I heard a lot of diatribe from Hanafi about who he was and what this cult was about. But I knew for sure that he would never leave it and that he also never prayed. It was a godless group dedicated to destroying life as we know it in our country.

Somewhere in the middle of April I came home to a message on my phone. When I played it relief flowed over my body. It was an agent from the FBI and he wanted to meet with me. He was calling from San Jose.

Early the next morning I was on the phone to him. When I heard the receptionist I again relaxed. I was noting to myself how often people made me suspicious of who they were. His voice was clear and sounded so wonderful, I felt like

I had been overseas and was coming back home to America. He wanted to meet with me in person. I felt validation for what I had endured. I was elated.

I arrived early at our designated meeting place and raced downstairs. It was the same plaza building where I first started writing and reciting poetry. In the restroom I brushed my hair twice. I knew I was nervous but I wasn't shaking. I dressed the way I always did when I was with my poetry friends, jeans, a sport jacket over a sweater, and tennis shoes. In my hand was the list of the Shubus of Monterey County.

When I walked up the steps I saw a tall man in a trench coat standing just inside the doorway. I walked up to him. He was very tall and lean and I had to move my head back to look up at his face. I asked him if he was Mr. George Thompson, the name the agent gave me on the phone. He said yes but didn't show any ID and I didn't ask for it. Later on I wondered why. I guided him to the coffee bar where we picked up our coffee. I didn't let on that I was hungry and my stomach hurt.

We sat down by the street windows. A lot of my initial fear from the ordeal was cracking away as we talked. He asked for my copy of the list and I handed it over to him. He told me that the leader of the group whom I had never met lived and worked right in the town we were in, that he had a travel agency and his name was Ashmael. His body trembled a little as he spoke these words. In fact, the man who was this group's leader had his business up on the hill, mentally registering that it was located on the way I go home.

I think we talked for over two hours. He asked me if I'd like for him to speak to Hanafi and I said no in a shiver. He insisted and said he would also speak to the ringleader. I looked at him and realized the fear I felt was for him. I didn't want him to go near them because they were monsters to me almost beyond the human level.

Then he pulled back from the table and reached into his coat's inside pocket pulling out a computer print out. He became very nervous as he opened up the paper and began to read it to me. I looked directly at him with all my concentration. I was glad he was nervous because it made him look human to me. He was reading about Kenneth "Hanafi" Feist who had been convicted in Monterey County of sexual molestation of minors. Hanafi was a registered sex offender.

George's eyes were blinking so fast as he read; it was difficult for him to speak the words. All around me was the crashing; the crash of a system that had allowed an organization full of hate to operate and harm people in the educational system. This deranged predator was allowed by intent to find me and frighten me. So much cooperation for hate and support of subversion from a system I had devoted my life to for answers and truth was souring on my face, in my ears. And it was done with a mission being heard around the world. The mission for the present was the announcement of the jihad, the call of the 20 nations, the total destruction of Israel and Christianity and our way of life in the United States through terrorism for the sake of terror, chaos. It was stupid and education was the target or one of them.

We finished our coffee and he paid the bill. I joked with him as he paid, saying that the video camera above us was recording everything we were doing. We laughed and then I walked away towards the back of the restaurant where our group table was located. George yelled something at me and I turned surprised at anything so spontaneous happening. I couldn't hear him so I cupped my hand to my ear yelling back, "What?" He said with a genuine laugh of good cheer, "Gabrielle, I look forward to working with you!" I couldn't help myself I was beaming all over, glad that he was there, and I warmed up for a few moments feeling good enough to smile back and wave. It had been months since I had felt anything this nice. Then he waved, turned and walked out. I sat down so glad it was over. He had told me to call him anytime I needed help or had questions but I knew I was finished. I wanted to move on with my life. He knew we were going to work.

Then overnight where I lived turned into a nightmare and I was told to leave. The wildness of the area came close to me during this time similar to the time the butterflies made me flee the danger on the coast. One night I was walking home from a musical event and as soon as I stepped into the moonlight I felt sick almost like a knife had been thrust into my side. Then after I climbed the hill I could hear the ocean roaring in the dark. Suddenly, the sound of clattering hoofs came up from behind me and I turned in a jerk.

There were three deer. They accompanied me almost all the rest of the way home, sometimes moving close and brushing up against me. They were my friends that night and I was glad not to be alone. Then I realized nothing would happen to the grim group of people I had met, the Shubus and Hanafi. No charges were pressed. Their lives went on and mine was disintegrating.

My fears were overtaking me and I was suspicious of everyone I knew. I began to think I was all alone and I was running out of strength. I called George telling him my mother's telephone number because I wasn't sure where I would be. Just calling the number and hearing the voice announce the Bureau tore the veil of fear that had descended over my mind. No one was exempt. How could all this happen to me? I was too tired to think any longer and I needed rest. I asked him if I was a target because I was a teacher? He had no answer.

I moved my things into storage when out of the blue my mother called me at the coffeehouse. Her voice was maternal like from an intuitive beam of light she said, "You sound ill. Why don't you come home for awhile?" I said no and hung up. As soon as I did I almost fainted. I called her back and said, "Yes, I need to come home."

I spent the next three months at home commuting with my sister and brother-in-law because I had no car. I often would wait at the cafe until midnight to catch a ride home with relatives working on the peninsula. The waiting was fun because I was with my cafe society friends and people took turns buying beer. It was healing for me because I knew everyone and we laughed and I could still perform. People seemed so kind and I craved familiarity. But underneath I was bone tired.

One night I was waiting in the restaurant where my sister worked. It had an open-air patio with an open pit fireplace. The area was dark except for a few flickering candles and the flames of the fire. There were only two or three people sitting outside like me. I was sitting in the dark shadows at a small table sipping an Irish coffee when I heard a ping and then I felt a large drop of water on my forehead. It was raining! I turned my face up towards the dark sky and murmured a thank you to God. It was cold and the rain was coming down steadily right into my coffee cup but I didn't care if I was getting wet, my God had answered my prayer. It was raining.

My birthday came around and at midnight my mother brought out a lighted cake and asked me to make a wish. I looked at her and said I wanted to be healthy. I looked at the cake and blew out the candles.

My parents left for a job that took them out of state. They would be gone for months. Several days I spent lying in bed in deep pain in my head. Nothing could stop it and it made me lay very still hoping for sleep and relief.

Then one night my brother-in-law came home from work in a rage, throwing things in their bedroom and the family room. In the back of my mind I remembered him telling me he kept a gun in the house. My nerves couldn't stand it anymore and I looked up in the phone book for an emergency number for women in domestic violence. I found one, called and they agreed to meet me at a secret location the next afternoon.

I packed my few things and ironically, my brother-in-law offered to drive me. I knew he didn't mean to be that angry. I told him to let me off at a store, which was a few blocks from where the lady would meet me. I had no idea what to expect but I was too tired to do anything else but follow the directions. My brother-in-law wished me luck when I got out of the car. I thanked him and watched him drive away like nothing had happened. I walked over to the appointed meeting place and waited. It was only a few minutes when a nice looking lady pulled up in a shining car and opened the door.

She spoke my name and I said yes and got in the car. Tensions were springing off me. I was so disoriented I could have been blindfolded because I didn't know where we were. In five minutes we were at a lovely bungalow in a quiet neighborhood. I brought my bags in and was shown a gorgeous room with brass beds. Then I was given a tour of the house. There was a large modern kitchen but best of all was a wrap around deck with a panoramic view of the ocean. I was going to rest.

The Gulf War ended and I was safe from Hanafi. I thought that was an amazing coincidence. I only remembered not hearing about it anymore on tv or from friends. One of my favorite coffeehouses went out of business. It was sad and it was the beginning of the end of an idyllic lifestyle so many people I had met had lived on the Monterey Peninsula. Bohemian existence with odd jobbing, waiting tables, bartending, part-time work, and then devoted hours to writing, painting, performing, reading, art shows, and wonderful conversations.

In the middle of all this turmoil in my life, one of my favorite poems that I wrote won a covetous first prize at the most prestigious arts foundation on the Peninsula. A call had come from a fellow poet friend of mine inviting me to the poetry reading where the awards were given. I bought a special outfit, hand painted on deep purple velvet for the reading. When I arrived I scooted around to the back of the room and took a seat. The third and second place winners read their poetry first. Everyone was looking around and whispering wondering who was the first place winner. Tears stung my eyes and my heart pounded into my ears when I heard my name as the first place winner and would I please come forward to read my poem, "Walk In The Velvet Woods". It was poignant moment for me. I felt the rallying of the Peninsula community when I was at my lowest and weakest. The prize breathed new strength into my life. I took the prize money back to my long time endearing friends who had supported and seen me through all my growing pains as an emerging poet. The money bought beer for everyone. I was celebrating the beautiful blend of people who lived in the towns along the marine life sanctuary. I knew I was moving on, so it was an appropriate good-by.

Walk In the Velvet Woods

Walk where the rattlesnake grass
Jumps up to greet the sting of life.
Walk where the mushroom sprouts
To catch the baby raindrops
To spin a Dreamland.

For my careworn life,
Walk by the cathedral of trees
As they bend low, shed their great jackets
To bare their souls to catch mine
As I fold into the rich earth.

Walk into the velvet woods,
Walk by the spinning spider's web
Full of dew, the newborn fern leaf
Under the winking stars.

Walk with me
And walk away to
Dreamland.

9

The Escape

○ ○

"I will not forget you!
See, I have engraved you on the
palms of my hands;"

—Isaiah 49:16

"For I will pour water on the thirsty
land,
and streams on the dry ground;
I will pour out my Spirit on your
offspring,
and my blessing on your
descendants."

—Isaiah 44:3

I had entered a haven, having no idea I was beginning a long journey to health. My birthday wish was beginning to come true. Living in a house that hides women who have been abused requires utmost secrecy. I was free to roam around during the day but at night the doors and windows were safely locked tight. No one could know the address except the residents and counselors. I began peer counseling with two lovely women who were near my age. They shared their own frightening histories and gave me some keys to lock and unlock the door to the terrors that were beginning to incapacitate me.

During this time I became aware that I was once vibrant and highly competitive. I received a rejection for an National Endowment for the Arts grant I had applied for but was accepted into a huge exhibition in France, the Grand Prix de Internationale de Paris. However, I was incapable of keeping the stride I had been accustomed to and let everything go.

One night I woke up around midnight sweating and fearful. A horrible nightmare had invaded my sleep. I got up and walked to the night counselor's office. It was one of my peer counselors. Her kind voice soothed over some of the immediate fears and she suggested we go sit out on the deck and talk. The autumnal air was lovely; the moon was out as I told her about the nightmare and what it meant. We talked for hours about the meaning of it, my fears, the terrorists, and then talk turned to art and poetry. She also painted and wrote poetry. I really needed her friendship that night and will never forget her patience with me. But underneath I was beginning to realize I was becoming afraid of people in general. I could piece together all sorts of conspiracies, real and imagined. The sad part was I couldn't tell the difference. I was losing my reality base.

I could only stay for two months in the safe house. I had started attending peer counseling sessions, which were conducted by a special lady who befriended me. The sessions were centered on abusive relationships. I learned about the cycle of abuse and how it had damaged my life. The sessions opened my eyes to the rhythms of my life. I got a job as a nanny and moved out to the family's home. I kept in daily contact with my friend and counselor.

The family I lived with resided in a beautiful upscale neighborhood. The house was spacious and I had my own bedroom and my duties were light. I was even given a car to commute in which I used to substitute teach or rather be the "teacher of the day". I only worked in the military schools so I felt safe. Within a month, right after Thanksgiving, the whole situation where I lived collapsed. The father was liquidating fast and moving out of the area because of some scandal he had been involved in had come to light through an investigation by local and state authorities. One of his friends was already in prison. The fears were flooding in again and my dear counselor arranged a rescue, packing me up in one morning and whisking me off to her apartment to stay for the holidays.

I planned to go to midnight mass on Christmas Eve but the flu racked my body. I spent the night in bed in a dark quiet room medicated with cold and flu medicines. I was so disappointed. I lay there thinking God was showing me that he could not stand me, that I repelled him, and that I would be lost forever. My counselor friend had warned me just before I fell ill that I could end up homeless. I know I didn't understand and that my physical misery matched the misery of my soul.

Then, through my fever I heard it. It was raining, no pouring. The raindrops were pelting the roof and window. Water for the drought! My little prayer was being answered and God was near! The comfort of this knowledge put me to sleep. I spent Christmas Eve wrapped in God's love.

New Year's Eve, one year past the blue moon fiasco and three years past my New York art opening, was a quiet little party with mutual friends from the network of help. I was out of the cycle of abuse, the graph of it indelibly burned into my memory from one of the counseling sessions. This was my defensive attitude, my thinking was clearing and my body was safe was all I thought. I trusted the people I was around.

One of the ladies at the party had a room for rent. She agreed to let me see it. I liked it and she let me take it. The location was great and I moved in that week.

I did not want to overburden my friend and counselor. I gave her my best miniature painting to repay her for all her kindness. She told me before I left that what saves her everyday is medication. She took a pill every night and was in bed asleep by 10 pm. She was a lady full of style and knew about improvising and odd jobbing. She was elegant in her attitude toward life but she had been through hell herself and devoted herself to helping other women out of the darkness of abuse into the light of life. I knew I didn't want to be homeless and practically scoffed at the idea. Certainly I couldn't see myself hanging by a pill every night.

I lasted two months at the new place. The woman I had met at the party and who rented me the room had a respectable job during the day but was a prostitute at night. Her pimp would call her up at midnight and she would slip out. I was really tense. I called the high school, which was two blocks away to report it. They said there was nothing they could do. American civilization was slipping away from my concepts of it. I was feeling very fragile.

One day I was sitting with friends in the cafe trying to figure out what to do. I had decided to leave the area. I knew the army base would be closing down and the economic repercussions from that would be far ranging. My poetry reflected this event like the apocalypse. I listened in the readings as other poets from around the area were writing on the same theme. I wasn't going to be able to support myself. From all the trouble I had experienced, my attitude on life by my beloved marine life sanctuary had soured. I needed to work full time and make more money and live better. I had decided to apply to UC-Berkeley's graduate school's writing program. In one year I would be eligible to add English to my teaching credential. I had never lived in the San Francisco Bay area and at the time it was part of the then California Marine Life Sanctuary to which I had been devoted.

I was sitting with my coffee contemplating how to move one more time when an old poetry friend breezed in affecting one of his characters. He was a French monk, Claudell, who was leaving the monastery to fight in the wars and had come to rescue an old friend. He was my knight in shining armor. The waitresses', who were young girls, mouths dropped open because he was very handsome and his manner was so dashing that he took our breaths away. I played along because I sensed that he had really come to rescue me. I waltzed out the door with him and then he quickly told me he could help me move, today if I liked.

We drove over to my apartment, packed up my few belongings and moved them into storage. I vowed it was the last time that would happen before I left.

I told my dear lifeguard that I had a place to stay for the two weeks I had remaining until I left town. I didn't want to worry him anymore. I told him about my plan to go back to school. He said he would be glad to move me to Berkeley whenever I was ready. I thanked him and I gave him money for gas. My things were stored safely and insured and now I needed to wait the few weeks until my next check came and I would be off, hopefully leaving danger behind me.

10

The Tent of the Lord

o o o o o o o o o o o o o o o o o o o o o o o o o o o o o o o o o

"Lord, who may dwell in your
   sanctuary?
   Who may dwell on your holy hill?"

—Psalm 15:1

"Now the dwelling of God is with men, and he will live with
them. They will be his people, and God himself will be with
them and be their God."

—Revelations 21:3

My things were stored and a friend surfaced out of our cafe society to offer me his
camper to stay in for the couple of weeks I needed until I would get my last check
before I left for San Francisco. I had begun to go to the local Catholic Church to
pray before the beautiful life size statue of "Our Lady of Fatima". My Irish Catholic grandmother had taught me to pray in front of her Mary statue when I was a
little girl and it was a comfort to me now. My friend, whose name was Paul, and
I spent some time in spiritual conversations. He was the offspring of a marriage
between a Jewish father and a Protestant mother. He wanted to take me to some
of the gathering places of his spiritual friends. It was the beginning of the opening
up of deep spiritual experiences shared with others. I wasn't alone anymore.

There were two groups. The first meeting I attended was held at night in the
basement community room of a local Protestant church. There were many
diverse occupations represented but all shared a unique common heritage and
bond through their evening service. These celebrants wore the vestments of rab-

bis and the language was in Hebrew. However, the content was from the New Testament with the main focus of the gathering to break bread together in Holy Communion. I felt the mystical pull of the early Christians who celebrated the Eucharist in Hebrew wearing Jewish vestments. It was a very moving experience. These were the Jews for Jesus.

Before we broke bread together there was a speaker who had just returned from Israel. He was full of the spirit and was trying to recruit others to return to the Holy Land with him. He gestured as he spoke of the closeness of God, that it was like he could reach out and touch the Lord or more like the Lord was reaching out to him. It reminded me of my wonderful rainy Christmas Eve. After the service, a kind lady approached me with a large loaf of the braided Communion Bread.

She gave it to me with a blessing for my journey. I thanked her and felt so happy to carry the Host home with me. The feeling of protection came back to me. I decided to celebrate with wine my leaving and invite my friends back at our coffee shop, which also sold beer and wine.

After the service on the long walk back home with Paul I realized that this group was very aware of the terrorists exposure I had recently been through. They had been so warm and kind to me in direct opposition to how the jihad instigators had been, who were like gangsters. The warmth of this little underground group was to comfort me in my memory, in my soul over the next few years. It was one of the shared places I was accumulating for strength.

My friend Paul was interested in what I thought about the service. I let him know how deeply moved I was by what I had just witnessed and the early Christian Church had come alive for me this evening. He said there was one more place he wanted me to see and be apart of before I left.

We walked maybe two miles back to his camper and said good night. He went into his apartment and I opened the door to the camper. There were no lights but I welcomed the darkness. I was warm in my sleeping bag and had many thoughts to work through before I was to leave. The air was warming up because it was March and spring comes early to the Peninsula. Sleep overpowered me and I was gaining some peace of mind from praying. I could feel my spirit; my soul was resting in a calmer place thanks to the prayers of others and God's good grace. It had been months since I felt peaceful.

The offer of the camper as a place to stay and being brought to this spiritually enlightening service helped me to trust my friend Paul. When he suggested we go to the other gathering, which was even more spiritual, I agreed. I prayed every day to Our Lady and mostly stayed to myself. I was going to be leaving soon and my energy was mainly directed towards this change in my life.

The next meeting my quiet friend would bring me to was held in one of the old historical Catholic Churches in Old Monterey. I looked forward to going just to see the Church. This meeting was held at night also.

When we arrived, people were spread throughout the Church. It was a very informal gathering and the leader was a doctor from the community. I knew who he was but we never exchanged greetings. Instead it was as if he was the keeper of the Holy Fire of God, and helped the Holy Spirit move through the people. People shouted out as they were moved in different ideas and thoughts.

The service was a Pentecostal meeting with people calling out from all over the Church with messages for whoever heard them with their meanings. I watched but knew I was not a part of this experience except as a witness.

However, towards the end of these energetic exchanges a lady was introduced to us. She was a spiritual healer who was blessed with the Holy Spirit. We were welcome to come forward towards the altar where she was standing. Paul urged me to go talk to her. I did.

She sat down on the steps that led to the altar and motioned to me to join her. She told me that I had been through a terrible and unholy experience but that God was protecting me. She told me that tonight God would give me a sign of His further protection as I go on my journey. I bowed my head.

This lady who wore a plain robe, her hair cut short, living the simplest life, put her hands on my head and began to speak in tongues. I had heard tongues spoken before and it had always made me nervous. But this night it was different. The whole area around her was alive with the language. Then she spoke to the Archangel Michael asking him to guard and protect me in my journey.

My head was still bowed but my eyes were open looking at the ancient stone floor. Quickly a red beam of light sped out of where the lady and I sat. The light stretched clear down the aisle and out the door. I was deeply moved and put my whole being into God's care. I didn't mention that I saw this light as it formed a cross at the bottom of the steps up to the altar and out the sides of the altar. My vision was peripheral as the light turned red and sped along the middle aisle and out the door.

Paul and I walked all the way back, probably five miles, but we were so energized by this Holy experience. I thanked him for bringing me to this meeting and again for a quiet place to stay. It was my last week on the Monterey Peninsula.

On Friday, a few close friends including Paul and I were sitting at our table. I ordered small glasses of red wine for each of us. I asked Paul to bless the wine and then we raised our glasses and drank it. I decided it would be my last glass of alcohol at least for a long time.

I had cashed my last check and packed a few things. I had already sent my application into the writing program and had a list of small hotels in San Francisco that were affordable. I said goodbye to my friends and I walked to the camper. I didn't sleep well that night because I was anxious about the future. Before I drifted off, a vision of a beautiful altar, appeared in my mind's eye. The Archangel Michael was in charge of it; he was showing it to me. I closed my eyes and went into a peaceful sleep. My path was chosen but my mood was of uncertainty. There was no elation that an adventure can create as I bought my bus ticket and boarded the bus the next morning. My faith in God was guiding me now. It was something new to me but I was in complete trust because I was beginning to feel a great strength from myself that I could do anything through faith in God.

Fortunately, my internal writing energy took over on the trip north. As the bus turned through each town and city on the way I was entertained by a mental narrative that described and laughed at the scenery and past and coming events. I had quit writing down my thoughts months ago in order to gain more discipline in presence of mind but the dry wit like a filter for life passing by so quickly was a welcome relief. There was no fear in me.

When the bus arrived in San Francisco, I was looking forward to my new choice in life. I quickly found a room in one of the little tourist hotels on Nob Hill. The concierge was very friendly and I paid him for a week's stay. He mentioned some places for me to visit and recommended his favorite, which was the Italian National Catholic Church or St. Peter's and Paul's on Washington Square in North Beach.

I spent my days looking for work, signing up with temporary agencies. The unemployment rate was dismal. On Wednesday I was sitting in one such agency's office reception area. I remembered it was Ash Wednesday. It was mid morning and all of a sudden I was stricken with nausea and my hands began to tremble. I spoke to the receptionist telling her I was not feeling well and would call to reschedule for an interview.

As soon as I walked out into the city air I felt better. I walked towards the hotel concierge's favorite place. On the way I passed a smaller church with people streaming in and out of its doors. It was a red brick building not particularly eye-catching on its outside except that the architecture was a rapid departure from the surrounding ornate Chinese architecture of Chinatown where it was located. I entered the church with the flowing human stream of the crowd.

Once inside the door I noticed some literature on one of the tables. There was a small chapel on each side of the vestibule. I moved towards the table and read the bold words on one of the brochures. It was about returning to the church, with a list of several reasons why people are alienated from church. I picked up the brochure and surged into the sanctuary with the crowd. It was packed clear back to the entry where I was. I quickly took a seat and kneeled to pray. My eyes wandered up towards the altar. There against the walls behind the altar were three enormous oil paintings. The center painting was a larger than life size painting of Mary surrounded by cherubs and clouds, her eyes heavenward.

On each side a smaller but life size painting of the angel Gabriel appearing to Mary and the other side the Archangel Michael battling Satan. Then my mouth dropped open behind my praying clasped hands. The altarpiece was carved white marble and was exactly like the one in my "vision" that I had my last night in Monterey. My vision had brought me comfort then and now I could sit before this sacred place on earth. I felt my faith pull me like a rope thrown out to a stranded mountain climber.

I had not been back to church, any Christian church officially for over ten years. I joined the slowly moving line of people waiting to receive their ashes. I was overjoyed when the priest pressed the cross of ashes on my forehead, my eyes lifted up towards the ceiling. I silently vowed to make this return to the church.

When I returned to my seat I read over the brochure. The analogy of someone like me, alienated from the church, was like someone living in the desert. I immediately thought of the vision out over the Atlantic Ocean when the water turned into a desert. I thought of the drought we were all in, especially there was Desert Storm and the jihad, my special desert. All year I was to be in this spiritual desert.

11

Devotions

o o o o o o o o o o o o o o o o o o o o o o o o o o o o o o

"Sing to the LORD with thanksgiving;
> make music to our God on the
> > harp.
He covers the sky with clouds;
> he supplies the earth with rain,
> and makes grass grow on the
> > hills;
He provides food for the cattle
> and for the young ravens when
> > they call.
His pleasure is not in the strength
> of the horse,
> nor his delight in the legs of a man;
The Lord delights in those who fear him,
> who put their hope in his
> > unfailing love."

—Psalm 147:7-11

My faith was to carry me through for the next intense few days. I knew I was running out of money and had no job in sight. The second to the last day of my hotel stay took me to the outlying Sunset district of San Francisco. I was still hopefully looking for a room and had an interview with a lady who was offering a small salary plus a room in exchange for babysitting services for her small child.

I walked out of the interview discouraged and wandered through the streets until I was in front of the Salvation Army. I was feeling desperate so I walked in and made an appointment with their resident social worker. Her name was Rebecca and I believed she was like an angel sent from God.

She asked me several questions and quickly ascertained that I was soon to be destitute. Her voice was so kind but her manner was very professional. She gave me food vouchers to a grocery store and wrote a reference for a spot in a local shelter. I was so scared and grateful at the same time. I thanked her and walked out into the late afternoon air.

I turned the vouchers in and got two plastic bags of food. As I walked down the street I thanked God for a warm place to sleep and the bags of food, each item was precious to me. It was a feast in the middle of the desert. I walked past a homeless person on the street on my way back to my hotel. San Francisco was littered with homeless beggars. She was tattered and dirty. I gave her one of my cups of yogurt.

When I got back to my hotel room I was ravenous. I hadn't eaten for a day and a half and sat down to a delicious meal. Food tastes 100 per cent better when there is hunger. I thought of myself as breaking a religious fast. I took a shower in the shared bathroom and went to bed. Sleep came immediately.

The next day I packed everything and checked out. I had seen other people being evicted with dozens of bags stacked in the halls. I was glad I could just leave. I took a bus over to the address Rebecca gave me. The shelter was in a factory building and was run by one of the local churches. They took what was left of my food bags because the rule was no one brought food into the building. I think I was already in a state of shock but it hurt me to lose my blessed feast. Then they led me into what was called a dayroom where there were sofas, chairs, tables, a television, and a piano. Several others were seated with bags and suitcases and I took my place in a chair against the wall, numb with fear. We had to wait until 4 p.m. to be admitted. If there was room we could stay. My fears kept bounding up in me and I kept fighting off the feeling I was entering a concentration camp.

Then a delightful young woman with long curly hair appeared in the room. She had two other helpers and she was talking to everyone telling us to come with her for an art project. She came to me and put a paintbrush in my hand and beckoned me along. My fear subsided as I marveled at the idea that I would be painting the very day I thought I fell into hell.

We were led into a well-lighted room where art supplies and tee shirts were stacked on a table. She told us to sit at one of the empty tables and the helpers would bring around supplies. We could paint on paper or make a tee shirt. I opted for the tee shirt. The paints were brilliant California neon colors. I did an abstract Jackson Pollack-like painting of the sky, the mountains, and the sea. People really liked it and my self-esteem was zooming. I still have my bright abstract tee shirt even though it is well worn and full of holes.

When we were done and had cleaned up we were led back into the dayroom. It was 4 p.m. A man entered and called out names to sign in. I was one. My gratefulness was flowing throughout my body. I kept seeing myself in my mind out all night in a big, dangerous city, maybe at a coffee shop or just standing or lying on the street with the other homeless people. It was terrifying and I had thoughts of being robbed, beaten, freezing, raped and murdered.

Now I was going to be safe in this big building. I signed in and was given a social worker's name to see tomorrow. I was in awe of how well cared for my little life was.

I wandered back into the women's dorm. It was an enormous room and took over at least half of the building's first floor. There were aisles of bunk beds and I found mine and climbed in, storing my things under the pillow and in a locker nearby. I had a lock with me so my things were pretty safe. I found the restroom. There were two large ones with sinks, toilets, and showers just for the women. I went back to my bed and laid down to rest, waiting for dinner to be announced.

Dinner was delicious and plentiful. The men joined us there and a prayer was said before we got our food. I was thankful to be alive. Later into my stay I would hear some men say they would rather be in prison with a warm bed and three squares everyday, not worrying about everything. I was startled by this idea. Sometimes when we had shower time I would be afraid we would be gassed, my self-worth was so low. There were so many of us, I wasn't prepared for what was happening. Later I would come to realize I was experiencing symptoms of extreme anxiety.

One of the programs we were in was for employment. The job counselor set my mind at ease when she said it was not a sin to be homeless. She repeated this often and my paranoia left.

I had an understanding social worker to whom I could tell all the ugly story of the trauma around knowing Hanafi and the weird cult of the jihad. She listened to me and reassured me and I began to calm down from the terror that had been instilled in me. She was also a Muslim and I could get a reality check anchoring me in a better emotional base just from being around her because she was so none threatening.

There was a clinic with a doctor and a nurse who visited the shelter several days a week. My social worker had me sign up for a general check-up. She also told me how to get a general assistance check until I could get my unemployment benefits, which had stalled somewhere. As I walked along the streets looking at dozens of homeless people begging on the sidewalks. I couldn't think of myself as homeless. I didn't understand why these people weren't being taken care of like myself. I lived someplace that was warm and clean and relatively safe. I had the care of social workers and medical professionals, I could eat twice a day and stay clean. Soon I would have some money.

I lived at this shelter for two months. In the first week a younger woman who bunked near me befriended me. Her name was Steffi and she was very religious and a Roman Catholic. She took me to the early mass every weekday at the beautiful old church down the street from the shelter. After the mass, the lights were turned down and we could sit amidst the saints' statues and beautiful Tiffany stained glass windows and pray. I learned to pray devotedly from Steffi. She taught me all about the mysteries of the Catholic Church that I never knew before or else showed me books to buy to study. I started making a saints' chain adding a medal to my necklace of the saint I was learning about each week. People began asking me for medals and how to pray. I was so moved during this time and I began to send prayer cards and medals to my daughter, Christina. I also started my return to the church, which meant attending classes at the lovely old church in Chinatown where I spent Ash Wednesday. On Sundays, Steffi and I would go to an early mass at the great cathedral and then I would go on to my church. She had no interest in belonging to a congregation and her studies were done in mail order classes. Her spiritual path was *Bible* studies and comparative studies of different *Bibles*. I learned a lot from her.

One of the sacred teachings was the scapular. She told me the Filipinos who attended the church where we prayed each weekday morning were devout believers in the healing qualities of the scapular. She said it could bring about miraculous healing. One day we were shopping at one of the Catholic bookstores and I bought the green scapular. We had it blessed in the great cathedral after mass and then I put it on. It had two plastic rectangles attached at each end of a green cord. Inside the plastic rectangular jackets were felt and cardboard pictures of Mary and St. Teresa of Avila. One of the rectangles went in the front, the other on my back. I prayed every day that Jesus would heal me. After a week I developed a rash on my chest. It would not go away. I thought I had found disfavor with our Lord and he was punishing me. Then my belief in the scapular deflated and I told Steffi that the plastic was causing a rash on my chest and I had to take it off. She said I should go to the doctor.

The clinic was really busy as usual but soon a nurse saw me. She was young and sweet. She told me her name was Angela. I trusted her so I told her about my rash. She immediately gave me a tuberculin patch test. After the allotted time passed for the patch to work I went back to the clinic. Angela ministered to me again. My patch test was a red, rough raised area of skin. I wasn't sure what it meant. She told me I had tested positive for tuberculosis and gave me a referral to the TB Clinic at the city hospital. I thought of my little green scapular and then I realized I could never tell how God will work.

At the clinic, my X-rays showed a small scar from when I had pleurisy in junior high school so it wasn't too late. They gave me medicine to take for a year that would surround and isolate the tuberculosis bacilli and I would never get sick. They had caught it in time. For six months I made a monthly trip to the TB clinic for x-rays or chest examinations.

I often thought about how I became exposed to tuberculosis. My grandmother had told me stories about whole families dying from it and being buried together. My Irish great-grandfather had been forced to sleep away from the family house because of his coughing from it and it later claimed his life. His son, my grandfather, had been exposed to it when I was a little girl but had been cured. One of the first things required of me when I returned to teaching in California was to take a TB test, which was clear. But teaching was probably where I contacted this dreadful disease because I taught many migrant workers' children. I still have my scapular and keep it in my *Bible*. It was my first sacred object as I began my return to the Church. My little rash patch cleared up by the end of my stay at the shelter.

One other miraculous event happened while I lived in the shelter. That lovely lady who put the paintbrush in my hand the first day I arrived, held art and drama classes one or two times a week. Out of these classes I developed a line of greeting cards. They were paintings of different scenes of the then California Marine Life Sanctuary. They delighted people and they pleased me too. I really started learning about small business and I realized I had developed a test market with the originals, which I gave away freely.

Not far from where I stayed at the shelter was a very special place, which was open to anyone who wanted to make something in art. It was a free art studio with free materials and space to work. I went there, often working in clay, pastels on paper and later painting on canvas with my own paints in my own style with the metallic powders.

One day I felt compelled to draw the scene that kept playing over and over in my mind when Hanafi showed the neighborhood and me some of his perverse behavior. I used bright but off color combinations of pastels. It was an eerie image and one of the more professional and mature male artists noticed what I was doing. I explained it was an encounter I had with a registered sex offender. He shivered. Later in the month, one of San Francisco's papers printed an article with a neighborhood breakdown chart of the locations of registered sex offenders in San Francisco. It was incredible because the number was enormous.

I was ready to start painting again and had my own paints, brushes, and powders after my boxes in storage had been shipped to me. I wanted to do three paintings. One was a tribute to God in the new mysticism and scriptures that I had become acquainted with during my return to church. The other was a diptych, which are two separate paintings that hang together as one.

I completed the diptych which had a blazing sun divided evenly in the center of the canvas, one half on each side. The figure of a praying flying angel was in the left panel; Mary holding baby Jesus and flying over the Sanctuary was in the other canvas. The total concept depicted my surrender of my life to Jesus while I was living on the Monterey Peninsula and again in San Francisco.

The second painting was my rain prayer. It pictured God on His Holy Mountain in the Cloud of Unknowing hovering over the ocean but near the beach. Behind his mountain are three huge rays of light, which represent my prayer to God to safeguard us from nuclear holocaust and to give us precious rain. I took the painting outside to blow the metallic powders onto the wet paint. After I was done, I was standing in the sunlight on the street looking at the glistening painting. I picked it up and tapped it onto the pavement. Blue paint spilled out under the mountain like water onto the clouds and the waves spilled over too. I was overwhelmed by what I saw. Here was my rain prayer in a living experience in art.

Then, to my astonishment, a man who had been leaning against a car parked in front of the studio walked over to me. He had a black boom box on his shoulder listening to loud rock and roll while I finished the painting. He had sunglasses on so I couldn't see his eyes. He began to speak to me as he walked over. Pointing to the painting, he said point blank, "I know what that painting is about! That's God on His Mountain and He's stopping the nuclear bombs!" I looked at him intently and in awe. I said, "You're right! It's also about praying for rain!" I didn't want to insult him by asking how he knew. He was nodding and smiling as he went back to leaning on the car. For me, the Holy Spirit had moved through us.

My painting was drying quickly in the sun and I knew I was finished working in this studio. It had been fun but I had outgrown it. I was in a gallery in an upscale neighborhood and had several friends who were serious artists. I will never forget my experience with that man though. He represented what I have always found when people see my work. They have strong reactions and speak their minds. The fact that he knew the nuclear concept in it startled me but that is what creating art is all about. I felt blessed to be present when someone could communicate what he or she saw in my painting. It was the first time I felt God's presence in my art and audience.

Within a few months of working in this wonderful free art studio a wealthy benefactor bestowed a large sum of money on it and they opened a swanky gallery in the Embarcadero which is a far cry from the Tenderloin where we created our works. I saw sculpture and paintings that I wished I had money to purchase.

One day I felt so elated by all these turn of events I wandered over to the basilica near the studio that the Franciscans ministered. It was very old and beautiful inside with old parquet floors. I sat down. The altar was very remote from where I was physically, in the inner city, the Tenderloin of San Francisco. Outside were heroin and crank dealers and prostitutes. People were destitute and disturbed. I learned about St. Jude here, the patron saint of lost causes. The Lord spoke to me that no matter how clumsy I, could always come to him. I felt inadequate because I was not trained in any old Catholic ways. I began praying for the Irish that day. Praying for their poverty, oppression, anger, for their peace, a way out of where they were. I prayed that their way was mine too. I was poor, oppressed, angry, and I needed peace and a way out. Could the Lord find a way for Ireland? for me?

I had come to the end of my stay at the shelter. My caseworker had found a place for me in what was called transitional housing. It was a brand new apartment building and had excellent programs and I could stay for two years. The rent would be only one third of my income. I was accepted and moved into a beautiful two bedroom, two-bath apartment. There was a lovely garden in the back with vegetable and herb gardens and a patio.

I was to spend the next two years sorting out what happened to me trying to solve the problems once I realized what they were. I sent Agent Thompson an Easter card hoping he would understand that the terrorists meant Christians as well. I never heard from him. I think I was out of his jurisdiction.

One of the most profound signs of God in my life happened after I moved into my new home. One day I walked into my church and went into the little chapel of forgiveness. I kneeled and lit a candle putting my prayerful hands on the rail. I asked Jesus and God to forgive me of all my sins and to change my life. I surrendered my life to Jesus Christ.

Later, at home, I was sitting on the couch in the living room. It faced east and there were three bay windows in front of it letting in the light and a view of rolling hills dotted with residences with plenty of sky above the terrain. That day I thought about how astrology had become a communication point for me, and how often I read my horoscope for daily guidance in my life. The moon was the outstanding influence in my sun sign and I thought about how the blue moon had been a power to those violent people I had met on New Year's eve that day when Hanafi had brought me to their party. As I spoke silently to Jesus God I rebuked astrology and just then a full moon began to rise over the hill.

As it rose I began to laugh lightly and joy entered my body. My soul was being set free from astrology. I saw in the white-lighted full moon, the moon of Abraham. God was the moon and the moon was laughing and Abraham was laughing. One of my roommates, an older lady, came into the room and saw me looking at the moon and laughing. She began to laugh too and I felt she understood what had happened. I looked at her and said, "I'm free!" She laughed again.

Not long after this miraculous experience, I had a chance to witness to my transformation through the Lord. One of the young ladies who lived in our residence asked me for the horoscope in the paper. As I handed it to her she asked me what mine said. I looked at her and matter of factly stated that I didn't read my horoscope anymore. My religion gave me what I needed.

The last job I had as a temp in San Francisco was working in the stock market in a bank. One of the counties in California went bankrupt overnight due to bad investments. It was a shocking experience and it turned out only one person, a man, was responsible. I went to church at lunch since it was nearby. I asked God for protection. I read in the paper later that the man who made the bad investments for the county made all his decisions through astrological influences and reading horoscopes. He went to jail. I felt blessed to be free of it and thanked God quietly. I wondered if secret messages were printed or given through astrology and horoscopes for deviate and manipulative control of our lives.

One of the services offered through my housing was visits to a psychologist. It took me six months to ask for this. I was tormented by nightmares and insomnia. My days were filled with looking for employment, volunteering at the church's bookstore and taking business workshops.

I developed a ritual at night to go to sleep. Lighting a candle on the nightstand at the foot of my bed, I read some from my *Bible* and after adding a beautiful pale blue and ivory alabaster statue of the "Queen of Peace" with baby Jesus on her lap and the dove of the Holy Spirit quietly laying at her feet, I would gaze at the statue and pray away the day. I tried to have fresh flowers there and finally at

Christmas was given a potted red poinsettia for helping to decorate the church. This plant stayed on my prayer table for the next year and a half until I moved. It was a miracle plant, staying red the entire time, which is botanically impossible. The red poinsettia, the deer in the night walk, the fluttering butterflies, and of course the wonderful sea otters, dolphins, sea lions, seals, and whales all are God's creation reaching out in their nature to show me or anyone who wants to believe that the Lord cares and is only a whisper away.

I could relax and go to sleep after these prayers but by one or two o'clock in the morning I was awakened, usually in a sweat, with terrible visions from my nightmares but grateful to be out of them. It was the final prayer every night, to be awakened if the nightmares occurred. Then I would return to sleep only to wake up with the dawn's light. Sometimes I would go out into the garden or read the morning paper at the patio table by the early light.

I faithfully went to my psychologist who was a Jungian dream specialist. Sometimes my dreams were predictions of things that would happen later. Sometimes my body would be asleep but my mind was awake and I could see through my shut eyelids. I was desperate for sleep, wanting the nightmares to stop. As we talked, he gave me insight into the possibility that the system could cause my fears, which would then be reality-based. He was acknowledging to me that there are enemies that work in our system who could perpetrate the calamities that descend on me. He thought it was beneficial for me to be able to recognize what causes my fears, which cause my mental and emotional distortions. It helped to reach this truth. But it was also depressing because systemic enemies lent an enormous power to the evil pursuing me.

Christine announced her engagement to a co-worker without ever telling me about him. His name was Michael and he was sweet. They had worked together for three years in the insurance firm that employed her in Oregon. I wrote to her about possibly a sixth month engagement in order to get to know him a little better and that maybe I could come for a visit to meet him. She was adamant about how they wanted to marry right away and that it would be too late if I tried to stop them. She also let me know how wonderful he was and how well they got along. I backed off, what could I do anyway; she was an independent, grown woman. They married before I could meet him. I wished them well. They bought a house right away and that placated me for quite awhile. I knew they did not want a mother-in-law meddling around in their first year of marriage. I was glad

Christine still could write to me. Letting her go was painful but it was easier to let her go to her husband who was a sweet and gentle man. I knew she would be all right.

One of the medical cures during this time, as I journeyed on my way to health, was to have my abscessed teeth pulled. There were three in all and the source of my extreme headaches. My doctor told me that the poison could go right to my heart or my brain and kill me. The last visit to the dental clinic was my last extraction. The first oral surgeon couldn't budge it. In the end there were four oral surgeons up on the table and my body pulling my tooth and each other. I could hear their sigh of relief when it was finally dislodged. One of the doctors thrust the tooth held in a pair of huge tweezers into my face and said in an astonished but triumphant voice, "We've never seen such an enormous tooth!" I felt the soft pulp area where it had been with my tongue and it was equal to the space where the two teeth could have been. I thought the tooth must be from some primitive gene I owned; my father's family was an ancient one. I was relieved to be done and out the door. Later, I began to realize my "fight or flight" chemistry was different than most people, operating on a more primitive level and powerful enough to get me through horrendous situations afterwards only to make me sick. My tooth was a symbol of my primitive nature that clashed in my body with my highly developed and educated civilized intuition and skills.

I found a job for the summer as an art consultant at one of the piers on the bay. It was strictly a tourist season job. One night I was alone in the gallery because I had the night shift and would close up. The door was always open and there were many tourists walking up and down the balcony and in the mall area below. I was standing by some prints when a group of three people, a woman and two men, walked in. They were laughing and talking. I took them through the gallery explaining the artwork. One of them mentioned that they were with the Environmental Protection Agency. They were biologists and were in town wrapping up the paperwork on the federalization of the marine life sanctuary. I was thrilled and stuck out my hand, which they each shook. I said I was really glad to meet them and I had been part of a cultural experience in the Monterey Bay area promoting the new protection laws. I was thankful I didn't burst into tears when they left.

I was working on getting my greeting cards printed and distributed and meeting these officials spirited me on. I had selected four scenes and wanted them printed on a watercolor paper cardstock. Part of my profits would help the non-profit organizations that care for the marine life in the Sanctuary, from the Marin Headlands to San Luis Obispo.

My art consultant's job was over at the end of the summer and I knew by fall that I was through teaching. I was retiring from it. One evening, in the apartment several women had gathered from the building to discuss employment, specifically management. I was the only teacher there. I explained that classroom management was setup a lot like a baseball game. There were 3 chances for misbehavior and on the 3rd your were out the door so the rest of the class could work, like 3 strikes and your out in baseball. Later in the year the "3 strikes law" was enacted in California and federally. Our crime rate has declined all across the nation. I felt like my search for justice in my artwork was coming to fruition.

I got unemployment and joined a volunteer organization at the state employment office. The group was highly organized and dedicated to finding jobs for managerial and professional people. I quickly rose in the ranks to a Vice President's position with four departments to run. The number of people who were members was a testimony to how high the unemployment rate was. We were packed solid at meetings. I attended Chamber of Commerce events, organized picnics and parties and networked with diverse occupational people. By 1993 unemployment was so high in the city that we tried to place hire me ads in the now famous Silicon Valley's leading newspaper. The paper refused us. Some people were able to land wonderful jobs through our club. I stayed there a whole year. I spent time encouraging self-employment as I learned more about how to get my own little business started. By the time my year was up my cards were beautifully digitally reproduced giving the quality I wanted of an original watercolor. The cards were placed in several prestigious galleries and bookstores and began to sell. I had taken workshops in computer graphics designing my own logo and knew this was my new direction. I just didn't know the destination yet.

One of the events I helped organize was a big picnic in Golden Gate Park. I had an experience that was to be a pivotal point in my psychological well-being. There had been a terrible shooting in the city and I had a terrible nightmare about it the night before it happened. The picnic was the weekend after the massacre. On the way I got lost and wandered through the park. I was growing afraid. Then as I looked up at the trees the leaves turned to pale green glass and the leaves tinkled together in the breeze. My hair was prickling up on my body and I was very agitated with fear. As I rounded a bend on the walkway, an opening broke through the trees and there were my friends and the tables set up for the picnic. Reality came rushing in and the natural rustle of the greens of the trees returned. I didn't tell a soul about my experience except mentioning that I got lost. I was able to enjoy the picnic but I saved this sensory distortion for my psychologist. It would add to my growing symptoms of psychosis.

By the time my two years were up in transitional housing I had worked on getting my health back and finding a new career, since I had retired from education. I had made the decision to let my life's work in painting, nearly 30 years of artwork, to be auctioned off back east. Then I changed the direction of my artwork towards a more natural approach but still seeking the beauty of life. I felt stronger but knew I was living with new perceptual distortions probably stemming from my traumatization of the cult encounters. I had a name for my torments. My psychologist called it post-traumatic stress disorder. I had to supplement my income from my business with temporary jobs but I had been given a raise so I could live on my salary, the sales from the cards were extra. I was moving on with my life. The Lord had answered my rain prayer and the drought was over. I felt I wasn't in a spiritual desert anymore.

I moved out to the Sunset district, the area where I first realized I would be homeless. Now I was living in a nice house with a view of the Golden Gate Bridge. My housemates were ladies my age who loved art and music and had grown children. I was working long hours and when I came home I would fall into bed. I thought my insomnia was cured but instead it was to take a new turn. I had a natural friend to help me sleep and that was the fog.

The fog in San Francisco is a daily occurrence as sure as night and day. It rolls in slowly from the ocean past the Golden Gate Bridge and over the Bay and most of the city. One must love this fog to love living in the city. One evening a friend treated me on my birthday to a lovely dinner in a restaurant on the top floor of a major hotel. I watched the fog drift in preceded by three rainbows dancing over the bay. I tried to scribble a sketch down on a napkin but it was impossible. The beauty of those moments was breathtaking beyond art.

Here in my new home I had a huge room with a fireplace to myself. I built up a goose down feather bed and quilt bedding to bundle into at night. As soon as the fog came in all sounds outside were muffled. But it didn't matter. The stress from my job caught up with me and I was to experience new sleep disorders. I was working long hours and would collapse into bed as soon as I got home. I would sleep deeply for a few hours and then wake so refreshed that I thought it was morning often taking a shower and dressing for the day only to look at the clock in disbelief that it was still the same day. It would take me several years to realize that I was suffering from heavy symptoms of stress related to my ptsd.

I took off extra days at Thanksgiving and flew to Portland, Oregon to visit with Christina and her new husband. I was further relieved when I realized that Michael dearly loved my daughter and that they seemed to have a caring marriage. I slowly quit attending my beloved church when I found out the priests who were my spiritual guides were leaving. I couldn't bear it; my old feelings of abandonment were taking over, causing waves of anxiety within me. Then one day I consciously made the decision to leave San Francisco and move to San Jose, to the Valley to pursue my computer program. Unfortunately, I did not know how sick I was getting.

The timely decision to move away came just ahead of a dark, nightly messenger that had entered one of my housemates' life. The doorstep was just outside my window by my bed. I was almost asleep when a man's voice spoke in low tones and a thick Middle Eastern accent. I heard my housemate's lilting voice answer. I rose up to listen. He was trying to persuade her to his views, that all of European aristocracy and that Arabian aristocracy were all communists and that Israel was the enemy of the world. He had a newspaper he wanted her to read telling about events in the world that confirmed what he said. He told her not to worry because there were many people who know and who are banding together to stop this atrocious conspiracy. I drew away into my downy quilt to blink away my fears. It was the call to jihad spilling out of this man's mouth. The man quickly departed from the house as my housemate entered and went immediately upstairs to her room. We had quit communicating for the most part but now, I would give my 30-day notice to leave.

I was finishing up some computer graphics, Internet, and electronic publishing workshops. One day as I made my path from the bus to class I got a terrible shock. There, laying on the sidewalk, in his modus operandi drunkenness and passed out was Hanafi! I couldn't get my breath. When I got home I called the police and asked if I could get a restraining order against him. The officer told me Hanafi would have to do something physical towards me; otherwise there was nothing they could do. The air was swirling around me. I hung up and called Agent Thompson in San Jose. I got his voicemail. His voice was so comforting and when his message ended I had calmed down. I told him Hanafi was here and he was on the street where I go to classes like he was waiting for me. I was scared. He never called back. My trust evaporated.

Post-traumatic stress disorder is often like a psychological war for its victims. I felt I had entered another terrible battle. But I decided I wasn't going to passively take it. I bought an inexpensive 110 camera and film and brought it with me the next time I went to my workshops. As I neared the entrance to my classes there he was; his face had stitches, his eye blackened like when his "brother" hit him that New Year's Eve several years ago. He was curled up in front of a store, moaning, and drunk out of his mind, and the sun was beating on him. I stopped and started snapping pictures. After the sixth shot, a young man stepped out of the shadows of the door of the store. He was big and fair-haired like the "family". He kicked Hanafi saying, "Kenny, come on, move, the lady's taking pictures of you." I took some more shots and walked quickly on a few feet, turning into the lobby of the building where my class was held. I was learning to defend myself and feel good afterwards instead of falling apart.

After I developed the film I looked closely to make sure it was Hanafi. Then I remembered the young man calling him Kenny. No one called him by his real name whatever that was. Then I wondered if he had made it out of the cult. But I knew it didn't matter, they had won and he would die on the streets.

I had been traumatized by the predations of the nefarious Hanafi Feist when he and his dangerous organization reared its hideous head at me in Monterey. I had talked frankly with a psychologist about it; how it wound like a snake within our systems. I had the comfort of knowing the FBI were investigating at one time. But now I was nowhere near anyone who would care. The priests who knew me were leaving. I was too tired to start over and too exhausted to realize how lost these enemies were. Now the enemy was at the door again thanks to my housemate. I was able to quietly forgive what was left of the man named Hanafi. It looked like he was at the end of his life and I didn't want him to haunt mine any longer. I was going to have a fresh start in a new city closer to my home and family.

I had quit thinking, becoming disabled right on my job when in the middle of the morning I couldn't alphabetize a filing system. I was afraid snipers were in the building opposite our building. I left the building in a daze but made it home. I rode buses for two weeks until I got hungry and ran out of money. Then I filed for unemployment. The people at work at the state office recognized me but I was a different me. I couldn't read very well, but I didn't tell anyone. Then I returned to my job club.

It was a miserable time for me. One of the state employees suggested something was wrong when he found me talking to myself at the copy machine. I didn't think anything of it when I saw a video of myself that was filmed for a mock job interview. I looked highly distracted, my eyes, unfocused, darting all around and rolling in my head. I thought later it was because my dear grandmother, who had been my watercolor teacher when I was a little girl, had passed away and I was stress out in mourning for her. The thought of prayer or going to church had been eliminated from my mind, crowded out by fear. The devil is a thief.

Miracles occur when the time is darkest. I was on my way to pick up my mail at the rented mailbox at the Civic Center one day. This was my business address as well. As the bus came to the stop, I made a quick decision not to get off but continue riding for a while. I knew I was getting more irrational but as soon as I made the decision, my mind was lifted and it seemed like a host of beautiful angels appeared above me. There was a silky sound of singing and then it was over. I rode several stops and then got off only to get on the bus going the other way. This time I got off at my mail stop and was walking up the slight hill to the building when I saw an official van and a crowd. They were gathered around a big box on the ground that had been blown up. I looked at the van again and realized this was the bomb squad. I heard one of those fearless men say that someone had left the box on the floor of the post office building. Someone called it in as "suspicious". They detonated it outside. It was all over. I quickly and calmly went into the building and picked up my mail and walked away as fast as I could. The memory of the angels was embedded in my mind and provided a special retreat from the ordinary and dangerous world.

I didn't know what was happening any more. I knew it was not just about me or who I was, which always seemed so insignificant. But I was an American, a Christian, and I represented our culture to these people who hated the USA. I knew I was being followed but I also realized the terrorism had spread and was devouring others around me.

I took my little unemployment check and took the train to San Jose, California. I signed up at temp agencies and my agency in San Francisco told me they were opening an office in San Jose and had a job for me. There was no job and I felt betrayed. I was trembling like a hunted animal. I had rented an apartment in a motel for a week in San Jose. The concierge was really helpful and compassionate. I had run out of food and remembered to write down the United Way number for help. I went to the white gleaming cathedral to pray. As I walked in a light ray bounced from a recessed area to my eye. To me, God was getting my attention. When I turned my head I was awestruck. There, sculpted in gleaming white marble was the Archangel Michael fighting off Satan and my beloved Holy Mother crowned Queen of Heaven with baby Jesus in her arms. I walked over and bowed my head. I could have collapsed on the floor but the strength of a prayer welled up from me and I lifted my head upwards to the gaze of Mary and Jesus over me. I prayed out loud that she would send me home. Somehow I was fortified for what was to come.

My right leg and foot started to have sharp shooting pains and there was a fiery rash on my wrists that I scratched bloody. I knew these were terrible symptoms. On my last day in my room I phoned the number. I was told to go to a place and wait which I did for a few hours. Then the lady at the desk told me they had no room and I was to go to a certain address where they had room. It was all part of the same organization and the other place was handling their overflow. I didn't care, I was glad to be able to go somewhere.

I took the bus one stop too far and had to walk back dragging my heavy suitcase, when I heard laughing and talking and a ping-pong game being played. I came to what I thought was an Italian villa or else a convent. They asked me to wait outside. There was another well-dressed lady about my age sitting on a wall, waiting. We talked a little but I couldn't take my attention off the happiness behind the wall of the little courtyard. Beyond through the barred open windows were men and women sitting around in a large courtyard laughing and talking and four people in the front playing a fast game of ping-pong.

After we went through a fast intake and sign-in, I was shown a tidy medium size dorm room with built in beds in the walls for ten women. There were three of us and I lay down exhausted. The evening light was clear. I had a thirty-day stay. One of the ladies said this was a really nice place and I could stay here all day. I was in a shelter for the mentally ill. I was free to come and go during the day, but at night it was "lock down" until morning which made me feel safe. I stayed for eight months in what I called the "Inn".

I was sent to a therapist who finished my diagnosis of ptsd, panic disorder and anxiety disorder. For the first few months I lost all direction and had no idea where I was or how to get anywhere. They gave me a psychiatrist at the end of this stay who gave me my first psychiatric medication. I got a grant to go to a community college and study computer graphics, the Internet and web design. I rented a room for a while and finished school. I was strong enough to go back to work and then I was back in the shelter. They took me off my medication and I was working everyday. I was pronounced well and had saved enough money to move into my own studio apartment. During this time my dear Christine announced the coming of my first grandchild. She was born and named Marie Christine. The advent of this child was a light in the darkness. Shopping for a baby put an innocence back into my life. They all came for a visit and shortly after decided to move back to Illinois to be near her Dad's family. I was crushed. They purchased a farm and settled in far from me. I wondered if she was afraid of all the horror accumulating around me. I didn't blame them.

There were no more lurking terrorists, no more psychotic hallucinations of evil, no more analysis of systemic breakdowns, and no more nightmares. I thought that God had saved my life and my soul and I would proceed with my life. It was a success story. But I was alone.

12

Christmas Prey

o o o o o o o o o o o o o o o o o o o o o o o o o o o o o o o o

"Yet a time is coming and has now come when the true worshipers will worship the Father in spirit and truth, for they are the kind of worshipers the Father seeks. God is spirit, and his worshipers must worship in spirit and in truth."

—John 4:23-24

I had worked hard to get my life back together. Looking back to my life in Monterey, I realized that I had the right idea about closing the door on my wild side. The reason it didn't work and a demon-filled soul like Hanafi could break down that barrier is because I hadn't asked Jesus Christ to close that door with me. Also I had a strong Good Samaritan streak in my life. I think that energy is one that influenced me the most in my involvement with Kenny "Hanafi" Feist. There was a serial murderer in the 70's and 80's, Ted Bundy, who lured his victims using the "good Samaritan" concept. I started a series of paintings dedicated to his victims back in Boston in my award winning body of work but it was too depressing to continue. The victims were in God's second heaven. I think I live continually in the grace of God who spared my life.

In San Francisco I asked Him for help, for forgiveness, for guidance. I was blessed with a deep spiritual life in a party-driven city. In San Jose I began to pray for justice and peace. This time I was asking with the Lord Jesus Christ. I wasn't prepared for how powerful the evil was that tries to prevent justice and peace in our lives, let alone love. But I continued to pray for strength as I looked at each part of my life that was crying for justice.

While I was really sick, my nerves had broken so that I wore braces on my arms because of carpal tunnel syndrome, and a cast on my leg from breaking it when a nerve snapped in my ankle, I attended school, all broken down. There had been enough money to join a health club and hire a personal trainer. He was a Navy veteran and worked with me on strengthening my muscles and healing my nerves. He told me nerves repair themselves and I proceeded with hope. Getting the grant and finishing school helped me with my need for justice so that I could proceed with my future employment. My nerves healing over and my body getting stronger were like an outward symbol of my inner strength becoming more powerful in my faith and walk with the Lord.

Finishing my coursework, I was up to date on where the Valley was heading technologically and in business—open competition, high-speed digitalization of data, and the Internet. I needed a powerful computer to hold my colorful and texturized artwork and multimedia products that I wanted to develop. Within a few years these computers were produced and affordable. I believe following the principle of open competition accomplished that goal. I had catapulted into the Digital Age with fervor, thankful that I have an inquiring mind, a need to learn and grow.

I found a good temp agency and began working full time on projects that were enabling the principles or goals I endorsed. I saved my money and moved into a large apartment complex that had a swimming pool, tennis courts, and a workout room. I only had a studio but it was enough for me and had recently been remodeled. My personal trainer had moved on but I kept my workout with weights and swimming and added bicycling. I set up a little prayer area on top of my dresser and prayed every evening for strength. I prayed about the abuse in my life every night seeking to forgive and to be forgiven.

For six months I was living a normal life again, thriving and free of medicine and therapy and on my own. Then I hurt my back at work lifting heavy boxes. The injury knocked out some of my physical exercise but I kept swimming often at night and in the winter since the pool was heated to 82 degrees. Gliding on my back and looking at the beautiful star filled night sky, I had hope my future was more secure. I was grateful to my Lord God.

My back injury started the spiral down. I began to be aware of my psychotic symptoms edging back into my perceptions. I began to look suspiciously at people at bus stops or walking on the street. I was afraid to go anywhere at night except to swim and even that stopped.

At home, during my prayers I would ask God for help. I began to wonder at why I was so afraid and why I could not stay strong. I had been able to move and relocate all over the country, exhibit my artwork to be subject to many international juries, constantly meet new people while the marine life sanctuary was being promoted, all without fear and trembling.

I could still plan on expanding my business to the Internet, to include computer graphic design, and complete development of my products which were extreme complex tasks involving highly developed analytical and creative skills. This part was my future hope as the grip of terror began to invade my existence.

I worked at temp jobs for about two years suffering two back injuries from heavy lifting. We worked on projects that I loved or believed in so it was easy to be a part of the teams. But a private hell began to grow around me as reality ebbed in and out of my consciousness. An unknown fear or was it imagined, paranoia, systemic? The evil energy was invading my prayer spot. Finally at my last job I broke down crying and was sent home. I went on unemployment. I went to the state office to see if I needed to pay for a tax on my business. They had just returned to their offices from a bomb scare. I didn't owe on a tax because it was an electronic business. I hurried out. I never saw the bomb scare reported in the newspaper.

It was close to Christmas and one of the temp agencies called me for a job interview. I was sent to the same company where my son-in-law worked only in another state. The company had recently opened this office in the Valley. I was on my way home sitting on a bus bench waiting for a bus when a good-looking man swooped out of nowhere and stood beside me. I was careful about strangers but this man was forcefully friendly. He talked on and on as we waited for the bus. He was not an American and had a thick accent. He told me he was from Bolivia. I brightened up a bit and mentioned that I had a cd of Bolivian Indians playing beautiful Christmas flute music. I had seen them in San Francisco when they were street musicians and selling their cd's there.

I noticed he could not respond to what I was saying. It was dead air. It was a cue to me. Ptsd operates often from cues out in the environment. I asked if he had heard of them but he had no idea. The cue became a trigger, fluttering my systems and I could feel an anxiety attack building.

The bus came and we boarded. He sat down beside me. He began to pressure me to come to my house. I was terrified. I thought about getting off at another stop in case he followed me. Then he asked for my phone number. All I could think about was how to escape. I scribbled the number down and held it out to him. My stop was coming up. He grabbed the piece of paper and I stood up to get off. He didn't follow. I kept walking without looking back, my heart pounding. I hadn't thought to give him a fake number. I was just glad to be rid of him.

The calls started. He made a date with me to meet him at the public library. I waited in the pre-designated area for half an hour but he never showed. Later at home I felt safe but my trained instincts were still strong to find out who this guy was. I wanted to ask him point blank. He made three different dates and each time he never showed but called later in the day to apologize and say he was there but must have missed me. It was stupid. I wanted to confront him and expose him because I thought he was a fraud. He told me he worked in the public schools and was studying mathematics at the local state university. The third time I went to meet him, I noticed the city police were in several places in the area. He never showed and it was the last time I would try to meet him. But he continued to call me. I think my ptsd makes me foolhardy.

The calls increased to constant harassment. I began to screen my calls through my answering machine. I sat in my apartment listening to his accent. One night I picked up the phone. I began to ask him questions. Was he Japanese, a Sufi, or was he Russian? He laughed nervously at each question. He thanked me saying I flattered him. After I hung up I realized I was close to the truth. I had worked for a doctor once back east that had a similar Spanish accent and was from South America. Then one day I was asked too print his curricula vitae. To my shock his real name was at the top and it was Russian. I never forgot his accent because it was clumsy not fluent and romantic like Spanish is spoken. My new tormentor had the same accent.

Then for the first time since seeing Hanafi on the streets in San Francisco several years ago my fears moved to touch each other, congeal and speak to me of a possible connection to the wild cult I had been exposed to at the beginning of the decade.

I called a friend to help me. I was falling fast and I would have to vacate my apartment and get back to my medicine and therapy. I was glad for one thing; that I could recognize my symptoms and knew what to do.

One night I woke up in terrible pain and I nearly fainted after I got up and felt like my heart was stopping. My left eye wouldn't open and I thought I was having a stroke. My eye stayed shut for the next several days.

I began watching an evangelical ministry on television in the mornings during the next few weeks while my lawyer helped me break my lease and I made arrangements to move. I was having a hard time accepting what was happening to me when all around me was the biggest business boom I had ever been near. The soaring success surrounding me reached a peak of at least 66 millionaires made every day. I was breaking down fast but the support network was there for me. I kept trying to bridge to it but I was heavily suicidal. I was having a relapse into my illness instead of surging ahead with my business. All my plans for my business were being dashed in front of me.

In the macrocosm I saw the world ending because of too many people and not enough resources. Technology had not solved the deep problems I was aware of and I thought it was too late. The same hopelessness came over me as when the vision of the ocean drying up came to me on the whale watch back in Boston.

I wanted to keep going but my body was heading downward into an abyss. I was holding on by a thread. I know now it was a toxic release of chemicals, hormones into my body with names like cortisol. My body could not produce the endorphins my brain needed to feel good about my life. I was chemically imbalanced again.

My brain was malfunctioning because of all the stressful triggers I had recently encountered. The religious shows I watched on television were helping me to hold on even if it was by a thread. I remembered my Mormon grandmother watching the Rev. Billy Graham's revival tv shows and my grandfather telling me when I was in high school that because these shows were on tv did not mean they were not real and sincere. We never know when God will act. The personal stories of triumph and healing over the darkness and sickness and the open prayer for people were so comforting. I am certain the television ministers kept me alive during this time.

It was a thread of light leading out of dark labyrinth. One of the shows was the 700 Club. I had a telephone number to call that was available 7/24 for a prayer. I bridged over and made the call. I remember saying something about it's hard to believe being in the middle of all this success in Silicon Valley but I was unemployed, getting sick and failing fast. I remember hearing the voice on the other end kind and full of holiness praying for my welfare. I was so grateful. I put down the phone and wept. I put my entire being into Christ's hands.

It was after this prayer that a window opened up for me onto the spiritual sky and I began to witness amazing events connecting heaven to earth.

13

Omniscient Prayers

o o o o o o o o o o o o o o o o o o o o o o o o o o o o o o o o o o o o

"I am the light of the world. Whoever follows me will never walk in darkness, but have the light of life."

—John 8:12

"In addition to all this, take up the shield of faith, with which you can extinguish all the flaming arrows of the evil one."

—Revelations 21:3-4

The world was crashing around me. My body was getting weaker everyday; my apartment was a mess leaking up under the carpet and under the tiles in my bathroom and kitchen. I thought God had deserted me because I prayed everyday and things were only getting worse.

I walked out into the complex on a bright winter morning to go to the drugstore a few blocks away. I remembered the first year when I had moved in, so full of hope for the future. There were people walking around the beautiful pathways, children playing in the playground. Tennis courts were always being played on and the pool always had swimmers. The gates were a special protection to me and only residents with electronic cards that opened the gates could enter or so I thought.

Now I was seeing a mess, not only in my apartment but the management was always tearing something up until no one was outside unless it was necessary. The workmen would often enter our apartments for work to do or shut off the water. I was paying close to a thousand dollars a month for this harassment.

I went through the electronic gates and shuddered. All my psychological and physical safety was evaporating. Life around me was closing down around me. No one was at the pool or spa or on the courts and barricades lined the sidewalks. Even the tall graceful eucalyptus trees with their welcoming oils wafting on the breezes seemed threatening. As I walked away from my home I had a fleeting thought of a prison or worse a concentration camp. My mental state was severe anguish as I got to the store just a block away. After I purchased my items of aspirin and the newspaper I walked out the door to hear screaming sirens as several police cars tore past. I looked in the direction they were headed but couldn't see a thing out of the ordinary.

The residences that lined the side of the street were fancy condos but that was where the police cars were heading. I shivered and walked briskly home, glad to shut the door on the cold sunlight. I turned on the television.

For one instant I was in the presence of the Lord Jesus. There were no walls and He was standing in heaven and near earth close to where the condos were. He was so near I wanted to fly there to join him. The television station flashed a news alert. After a high-speed chase, the police caught the bank robbery suspect. He had shot himself outside his home. His home was in the condos up the street. The newscast went on to say the dead man had painted his face and body red and had shot off flares as he led the police in the chase to his home where he shot himself.

I was spiritually witnessing a judgment. In another instant I turned my life away from the deep chasm of suicide. I didn't want a demon taking over my life. I wondered if the man had been consumed by the demon that I felt hovering around my life, pulling it down. I knew my prayers were protecting me, there was a more powerful war going on than I had thought. And there was more to come.

It was February and the weatherman on the news was talking about a blue moon. It startled me. I was so thankful to be free of those astrological superstitions, but I had a fleeting image of the last blue moon I was aware of, at the violent New Year's Eve Party outside of Modesto.

I knew my body was sick and my soul was saved. I believe my ptsd is caused by my adrenaline gland producing too much of the flight or fight hormone called cortisol that protects us in dangerous situations and otherwise helps regulate our metabolism for life giving energy. It was powerful and it is what helped me stay in Hanafi's studio to get information for my country. The cortisol was now producing at toxic levels and soon it would be depleted. I was full of poison and becoming chemically unbalanced. My prayers were all that was protecting me now. In the next few weeks I was to become a prayer warrior.

The television was on, three women tourists were missing in our beautiful Yosemite Park. I mentally linked to this event and the horror of the events at the beginning of the decade was speeding by my mind in all its fearfulness. I picked up my *Bible* and opened to the first chapter of John. My mind was crying for God. I wanted him to help me, to help these women, to help all missing people. My brother was one, having lost contact with anyone in the family for the last four years. There was a young girl who had been missing in the Monterey area for over a year. She had a name similar to my granddaughter. I prayed for these souls. The Catholic Church had taught me that God was Lord of the missing, the disappeared, of souls already departed from earthly reality and of the unborn. I prayed for my father's soul. He was killed in a horrible car accident when I was a baby. I could be general and specific. I knew I was at the bottom of my life with nothing here on earth left to lose but everything to gain and if I lost I would fly to Jesus. I had very little self left, all my ambitions, my plans and the future of the earth was gone from me when I began to pray. I started from the beginning.

It was night. There was so much fear in me I felt it surrounding me in layers in my apartment as well as impacting my body and thought processes. I was sitting in the dark with just a candle lit at my prayer area. I read the first five verses of John, "In the beginning was the Word..." I dedicated my prayers to the Word of God. "All things came to be through Him, and without Him nothing came to be." I spoke in prayer to God in the dimly lit darkness.

"Lord, you created everything, the earth, the fire, the air and the water. Lord, You are the earth, You are all the earth. Lord, You are the fire, You are all the fire. Lord, you are the water, you are all the water." To me all the earth was sacred. In my small microcosm of life, I had consecrated all the earth and elements to God. He would answer me now.

As soon as I spoke my prayers, peace began to replace the fears, layer by layer and by the end of my prayers I could breathe easier. Then the miraculous occurred. The answers were tragic but they surfaced. The young girl's body missing in the Monterey area was found in the earth. For some unexplained reason it was found in an area which had been thoroughly searched. It was sad for the family but now they could bury their beloved daughter. I still was to wonder where my brother was.

Then the bodies of the three ladies were found, two had been burned in a car and the other left in a secluded spot of earth.

The water was my rain prayer, which has been answered every year since I started this prayer. The air was disappearance itself. There were two women college students were missing in the southern part of the Sanctuary. I prayed for them and for my brother and for all missing people. Their murderer has since been prosecuted and sentenced.

I needed God to answer my prayers for the families, the communities and for myself. The demon fears were backed off from me and I could finish the business at hand of packing and moving and to stand up in court to break my lease legally because I was disabled and could not afford to live in the studio any longer. To move on to where I had no idea. I needed to trust that God was close at hand. I asked Jesus to take the heavy burdens off of me. My back felt like it was literally breaking from the loads of work, the American dream of getting ahead, of being successful. The good parts as well as the bad were weighing me down. I put my life in Christ's hands and trust into the support groups that had become involved from my friend whom I first called to the mental health system in my county, to my attorney who would have to battle to free me from an apartment too expensive and also stress-filled with its constant repairs and the management too greedy to understand.

Christina beamed in like a ray of holy light. My son-on-law called me the last month in my hellish home to let me know I had twin grandsons. I was elated. I had known the twins were expected as my world collapsed and my Savior picked up my cross for me. Their gift of life was a rainbow. After I was assured all was okay, and my beautiful granddaughter was experiencing the wonder of her brothers and excited about being a sister and helping mommy, I walked outside to see the bush by my walkway had turned bright red. For me, it was a sign of God, His burning bush, His laws, and I was in Exodus. He would be with me the whole way; we would walk together, because we had a covenant. The babies were given

Biblical names. I went to the Church's gift store and purchased name scrolls for them.

I called a prayer counselor at the 700 Club to pray for me as I was hurtling towards the finish of moving. I settled in court having enough on deposit plus paying out of my savings. The movers were late and went to the wrong gate. The driver said he used his grocery card to let himself in the electronic gate. He was looking at me and laughing until I was laughing too at the folly of thinking I could try to be secure. We made it out, everything was stored and I went on a waiting list to re-enter the Inn. I had enough money for a motel room for a couple of nights and that's how long it took me to get into the shelter. It was Easter, the season when I was baptized, when my daughter was baptized, the most Holy time of the year. The anxieties of the last few weeks and growing psychotic break were calmed for now. Jesus was reaching out to me.

One of the joys of this time and one which I reflect back on, was the prayers of the lost cause I prayed for in the Tenderloin. The news was that Ireland had made a reversal of fortune and was now suffering the problems of modern culture such as pollution. I had to laugh. The dark days of poverty were over thanks to software engineers. St. Jude is the patron saint of Cupertino, CA, one of the major cities of Silicon Valley and I was living next door to it. My hopes were ignited with this miracle for the Irish. I felt pinned to this prayer. Now for the second half, myself out of the darkness, into the good life God intends for us.

My mind was disintegrating. I knew I needed medicine. Help was coming; I needed to hold on a little while longer. When I couldn't, the Lord held on for me. Together we entered the shelter and He was already there.

In one month I received my medication from my doctor. My asthma, I noticed always increases when my ptsd does. I received attention and medication from the free clinic in the Inn for it. I applied for and received state disability insurance benefits and to my great delight, I found a place to live.

I was in and out of the Inn within a month and a half. I found a place in a beautiful home out in a country town away from the noise and stress of a large urban area, which is one of the worst places for people with ptsd to live. Before I had chosen to stay and live in San Jose because I did not feel confident about my health in case I needed the support services. I also saw an attorney to apply for

Social Security Disability Benefits. My lawyer looked at me after I told him my work history and said, "It's time for you to retire." I nodded, my mouth unable to speak. I was granted what is known as retirement disability. I had worked long enough to qualify for the Social Security. I thought that is something at least. There was no reward from the government; there were no benefits from any business that had employed me.

While I was in the shelter I wrote a letter to the office of domestic terror at the FBI. I was finishing my prayers now asking for justice. I wrote about the phone harassment and profiled what I believed was a terrorist, giving them all the information I knew, that education was a definite target. Then I asked for a reward because they had asked me to stay and gather information on Hanafi and the Shubus and the call of the jihad. I asked because I had been injured and it was beginning to seem like it may be permanent. I had received a psychological wound I did not know was possible. A wound that carried its own war and infested my body; a wound I will have the rest of my life.

I got a call from an agent in Oakland and he arranged to meet me in a restaurant in Santa Clara County. I went there and waited an hour. I walked around in the restaurant looking for him. When I realized he was not there and not coming my old fears started to invade my body. I quickly left the restaurant and area. I thought I might be in a set-up; there could be a drive-by shooting.

When I returned to the Inn, people were talking about a terrible shooting in a high school in Colorado. Many students had been killed. It was the Columbine massacre. I never heard from the FBI again. I was right about the target being education. Later, in my own county, a young would be bomber was stopped before he could wreak his carnage; stopped by his own foolishness of photographing his weapons, then trying to develop the film in a commercial business. The lady who identified him now has ptsd, so does 25% of the people of Israel.

I could hardly wait to get to the country. There were songbirds instead of pigeons. It was deeply quiet at night even though the freeway wasn't far away I couldn't hear it, not like at my old apartment. I was in independent living, which meant I could care for myself, shop and cook my own food and no one would tell me what to do. There were several others living with me which is what I needed since I couldn't live alone.

Soon I switched my support team over to the private organization that ran the house. I had a new doctor and caseworker. My doctor changed my medication, which I may have to take in low dosage the rest of my life, but it works, for me it's a lot like heart medicine. Now when stressful situations occur I ride it out like surfing the waves. My doctor reassures me that my anxiety is stress related which activates my adrenaline gland to secrete too much cortisol into my body which in turn causes my brain to become chemically imbalanced. I don't get the endorphins that make us feel good because my nerve endings to misfire and that causes my psychotic symptoms to appear. My medicine is increased or decreased according to how anxious I feel. Knowing the physical side of how my illness works and how the medication acts on my symptoms has helped me feel I have some control and will not become a hopeless vegetated victim locked away in a sterile institution.

To face the stressors of my life is another story since that involves the big world. The jihad against Israel and Christians and America has increased to surprise massacres, suicide bombings, imprisonment, torture and executions globally. I am thankful to be a citizen of the United States when I read about these persecutions because the roots of our freedom our based on the protection against those aggressions. We experience trespasses against our rights and debate what that means but we come to a peaceful agreement in the end. We want others to enjoy our freedom as well. I want my freedom.

Sometimes freedom came to me in my own backyard. For years I have wanted to quit smoking. Many programs and cessations later I walked out into my backyard on night to a breathtaking night sky. Low gray clouds were circled over me with a hole in the center breaking open to the universe. It was like looking up at a natural dome lit from within. The presence of our Father God was so profound there were no words in me. Spiritually I let Him know that I wanted to stop smoking for good. He let me know to ask in His Son's Name, when I want something. Then I asked for my brother to be found.

Within a few days I found a state sponsored program for smoking cessation that was free and included a phone counselor. I signed up. One night when I was out smoking my last cigarette I could here my brother's voice saying, "It's not life, you know. Choose life." I haven't smoked another cigarette but the wonder or miracle is that the desire or addiction is gone. The most wonderful miracle is that my brother showed up in Colorado for Thanksgiving and we all had a nice reunion phone call.

I have my prayer table, my *Bible*, my 24-hour prayer telephone line with the 700 Club with its constant promise of help through prayer or prayer webs online. I look for more Christian music to help soothe my frayed ends. I look for a community to pray with in person. I can live alone again and have moved on to a happier place where there are no memories of terror. I'm painting again and writing although my ability to read an entire book a week is gone. (I had a voracious appetite for reading and was widely read.) I can listen to some audio tapes but that is rare. I scan newspapers and magazines and read off the Internet. I am blessed because my hands aren't crippled up and I can surf the Web and do research there. I have read and reread the website pages on American Post-Traumatic Stress Disorder for the latest information on how to cope with this disorder. I can meet others online in chat rooms and share ideas about myriads of subjects. I have an Internet business that offers Internet business solutions and products, web design, and sells my cards and gifts. My graduate school added me to their business mentor list for other students. I was selected as a member of Who's Who in Executives and Professionals. The drought in central California where I live is still at bay and southern California hopes to buy our water. My "Rain Prayer" hangs as a painting in my home always inspiring me. It is a whole unique prayer experience and anyone who has seen it never fails to ask me what the painting means, often offering his or her interpretations. It is my delight to share with them the Rain Prayer.

14

Post 9/11 Revivals

o o o o o o o o o o o o o o o o o o o o o o o o o o o o o o o o o

"There is no fear in love, but perfect love drives out fear…"

—*John 1 4:18*

"Nothing will hurt or destroy in all My holy mountain. And as the waters fill the sea, so the Earth will be filled with people who know the LORD."

—*Isaiah 11:9*

"Behold He is coming with the clouds,
  and every eye shall see him,
   even those who pierced him;
     and all the peoples of the earth will
  mourn because of him.
            So shall it be! Amen"

—*Revelation 1:7*

There is irony in the tragedy of the World Trade Center. The world has become painfully aware of what had shocked me into a traumatic disorder ten years earlier. Because of the awareness, my life feels more acceptable again, my alienation from my country has lessened. In the ten years since the "call of the 20 nations", information puts that figure between 60-90 nations worldwide that have jihad participants. The terrorists group are shadowy in substance and merge and submerge within their surroundings, ready from a cue higher up in command to hurt someone. As my country unifies against terrorism I feel wellness welling up in my body. We have to correct past mistakes. If we believe in our own values then we

have to have them represented in the world. We as a nation do not tolerate terrorism and are in a war against it. How long it will take to eradicate terror is to me
part of prophesy and up to God. In 1991 there was the Persian Gulf War with
Iraq and the beginning of jihad. Ten years later we are in a larger scale war or
containment against terror. We are in terror alerts in our country for all to see in
our colorful charts that pop up announced on tv and the internet. We are also
stopping at last the horror of the Iraq regime that signaled the first jihad I experienced. For me, I am in a replay only magnified now, easier to see and understand.
In 1991 I didn't know what hit me or why. Now I do. The World Trade Towers
destruction and the other plane hijackings were no mystery. I want my story to be
a light for others who have been hit or who wonder why.

Jesus seems so close to us. Evangelical ministers are proclaiming with the terror is the Second Coming of Jesus Christ soon. We will be with Him! The rally of
support for the victims' families, the heroism, the defense was so gratifying to my
body aching in toxics, to my soul. My isolation caused by my own traumatization
was breaking down. I thought this would be the focus of a huge revival across our
country. People were picking up their *Bibles* to read and gain spiritual comfort,
turning to prayer for guidance.

I had written this manuscript before the tragedy of September 11, but post-
poned trying to publish it. Instead, I was completely in awe of what was unfolding in our country and abroad as our population became aware of the jihad and
as our government responded in our defense. My alienation from my country
and the stigma I suffered from in my psychiatric disorder within society was so
intolerable to me. I often thought those two concepts were the main reason I was
not recovering. Now I was experiencing wellness, like turning the corner and
finding a familiar neighborhood. My story isn't about the jihad but about a call
to prayer, to come close to God because He loves us. I came close in prayer,
learned to be humble, learned to forgive and ask to be forgiven, learned to ask for
what I needed, met new people who were praying and I still am praying and
learning and meeting new people.

The mayor of New York was so inspirational to me. I had spent my adult life
looking at New York City as the ultimate goal for my artistic career since it was
the art center of the world. When I "arrived" in 1989 in a group show and gar-
nered several international juried awards for my body of work, I was so offended
by the speed of life, which was due to indifference and the filth and crime. Look-

ing up at the buildings from the street, I knew my work did not belong in that city. Suffocating in the pollution and darkness, I gladly left the city, not spending 24 hours there. I had made a conscious decision to leave for California instead of being swept away in the lure of fame to the filth and crowdedness of NYC. It was a huge disappointment.

Astonishment was the order as I watched on morning television the clean up of Times Square and New York City. A dead city had come to life before my eyes. The tragedy of September 11, 2001 was dearer because of the effort of this city to clean itself, to leave the path to the Babylon of Revelations and join the life waters of real community. There are several places in our country that are part of the evil Babylon the Book of Revelations mentions. But there are many people who work to stop the wages of sin and preach the love of God and salvation and redemption with Jesus Christ, our Savior. Our country has a sweetness and poignancy that is inherent in a majority of people believing in truth and freedom and who are willing to defend principles that our Lord wants us to live by for the good life he intends for us.

Politically, I sensed a revival when a man in my state of California challenged the Pledge of Allegiance's phrase, "under God", wanting it to be stricken in the name of religious freedom. The polls rallied, as did our legislature and now God will be on trial in the justice system in the Supreme Court. Once and for all to know and for good, His truth shall set us free. He is by our side! He is our defense. The terrorists would love for our country to leave the love of Jesus and protection of God.

Ministers have been disappointed that there was not a great revival in the aftermath of our tragedies. There were several in different sectors; in the open mourning for our national tragedies and the pouring in of relief money; for our troops leaving their families for our defense, taking over where police, fireman and civilians had battled. The musicians have written deeply moving songs to commemorate our losses and unite us. But the great turning to God is in the future. The United States has been through a great sweep to prepare for the Second Coming of our Lord. Prophecy says that there is a worse time ahead for the world before Christ's appearance. Now we pray more, we read our *Bibles* more, we give money to help the needy, and we encounter the Lord and welcome him into our lives more than before our shared tragedy. We are being prepared for this coming time. The end of the old age is over, the millennium is here and now we are hurtling towards the final battles of good and evil. The Lord is coming and we will be ready.

We are in a major time in history and Biblical prophecy. If nothing else throughout our turmoil as our country comes under terrorism's uncertainties and horrors, and as we flush it out of our midst, is the fact that God is steady and sure and that He loves us. If we pray to him, he will surely be there.

"Blessed are those who are persecuted
because of righteousness,
for theirs is the kingdom of
Heaven."

—Matthew 5:10

Epilogue

o o o o o o o o o o o o o o o o o o o o o o o o o o o o o o o o o o

"In him was life, and that life was the light of men. The light shines in the darkness, but the darkness has not understood it."

—*John 1:4*

"When I shut up the heavens so that there is no rain, or command locusts to devour the land or send a plague among my people, if my people, who are called by my name, will humble themselves and pray and seek my face and turn from their wicked ways, then will I hear from heaven and will forgive their sin and will heal their land. Now my eyes will be open and my ears attentive to the prayers offered in this place."

—*2 Chronicles 7:13-15*

When I pray, I pray for myself, for my family and for my country and the world. I pray for God to guide our leaders and for justice. I pray for my neighbor to be friendly and try to understand me a little. I pray that crime will stop, that there will be no victims. I pray for the end of terrorism. I pray that God will protect our military men and women around the world and our intelligence personnel who work constantly to end terrorism here and abroad. I pray for our citizens to stay strong and aware and to do what is right for our country. I have often been told growing up in our society that life here on earth would be close to life in heaven but that is impossible in our sick society. Now I have new hope for the human race, like our resources in renewal, that abuse will end. The possibility of peace on earth is coming, that our world will be a wonderful place for life the way the Creator wants it, a planet of love and life, not hedonism but the genuine deeply felt love between man and woman; love for our family, our children, where they are safe from harm; love among neighbors and friends, love for our planet, the animals and plants, the seas, the beautiful air.

I could stand on a rooftop in San Francisco and feel the heavenly city, the New Jerusalem, hovering over the sparkling American city, where on a street corner a man wears a sandwich board proclaiming it "Babylon" and lists all the hideous sins within, but where I found my Redeemer.

I could watch on television, the transformation of a dead New York City into a vital city of neighbors and interesting people, and where extraordinary heroes live. I can be a citizen of a state and a country, where little women and children were being kidnapped and brutally murdered. Where a population galvanized to enact child protective laws like "Megan's Law" and "Amber Alert" and children are being rescued before their demise and perpetrators are being discouraged with stronger punitive measures. A country where men and women will voluntarily leave their families to go to far away countries to protect us and to find the villains who would take away the Redeemer, and His life giving words and who would make slaves of us. Not where children blow themselves up for which their families are paid a ransom, or where plans are made to war against civilians at work because they do not agree with their religion or leaders or their freedom. We live with more awareness now and in a time where our country has become precious in its values and where we must put a stop to this darkness that wants to invade our light filled minds and hearts. One day we will not live in defense either but in love and peace and joy.

I am blessed by a state of grace. I gave up my life's artwork to live to see the meaning of that work be incorporated into our society from environmental concerns to victims' rights to the horror of the threat of winter white conditions of a nuclear holocaust become lessened as we try to take down our nuclear weapons. There was nothing more meaningful to me than to have the themes of my artwork addressed and solutions worked on throughout our country and the world. To be apart of life in this way was worth all the loss and hardships.

Being part of the research and the breaking down of social barriers that is happening in the arena of mental health in our society is really gratifying. Sometimes the mental health system itself seemed to be the problem to solve but most of the time it held the answers. It was the place where I could contribute my understanding of my symptoms of my disease and how to cope with it.

The meaning of my artwork emerging into society and the work in mental health has made my hellish decade worthwhile. Also work and research in education around the Internet and the computer tech world has made it possible for me to see a light at the end of the tunnel for being self-reliant. They were not my plans but I like to think in my wonderful relationship with my Lord, that they were important parts of God's plans to which I became a contributor.

Energy alternatives emerging as important issues in our society in the new millennium has been the environmental dream coming true. Solar, wind and now hydrogen power not only will improve our air and water quality but also will change the way we trade on the world stage and our relationship with the oil countries of the Middle East.

> "but those who hope in the LORD
>   will renew their strength.
> They will soar on wings like eagles,
>   they will run and not grow weary,
>   they will walk and not be faint."

— Isaiah 40:31

Biography

Suzan Michele Powers is an internationally juried and exhibited artist and published poet. She has a Masters degree in art education and has taught school for fifteen years in several parts of the United States. After having worked in business for over ten years, she maintains a small business on the Internet. The author currently resides in California. Her website address is: www.starbellenterprises.com

Bibliography

All quotes from the *Bible* are from the <u>NIV (New International Version) Study</u> <u>Bible</u>, Zondervan Publishing House, Grand Rapids, MI 49530, USA, 1995.

0-595-27670-9

LaVergne, TN USA
27 April 2010
180754LV00004B/152/A